Luca focused his dark eyes on Annah. "You have nothing to fear," he said, his voice smooth and conciliatory, yet he still held her wrist as if he didn't trust her not to reach for a sharp object. "I just want to talk."

Annah put her shoulders back. She would not be lulled by chiseled good looks, a crushed-velvet voice and thick-lashed, espresso-colored eyes.

She was stupid to have made that mistake once in her life; she wasn't going to make it twice.

Only one thing mattered right now, and it had nothing to do with Luca's magnetism or the tingling heat of his touch and everything to do with protecting her son.

"About what?" she said.

"Our son." His gaze held hers, challenging her to look him in the eye and deny the truth.

Annah swallowed. Her throat felt tight suddenly, and her eyes pricked with tears she couldn't explain. She blinked them away. "My son," she said, surprising herself with how ferocious she sounded.

Secret Heirs of Billionaires

There are some things money can't buy...

Living life at lightning pace, these magnates are no strangers to stakes at their highest. It seems they've got it all... That is, until they find out that there's an unplanned item to add to their list of accomplishments!

Achieved:

1. Successful business empire.

2. Beautiful women in their bed.

3. *An heir to bear their name?*

Though every billionaire needs to leave his legacy in safe hands, discovering a secret heir shakes up the carefully orchestrated plan in more ways than one!

Uncover their secrets in:

The Italian's Unexpected Love-Child by Miranda Lee

The Baby the Billionaire Demands by Jennie Lucas

Married for His One-Night Heir by Jennifer Hayward

The Secret Kept from the Italian by Kate Hewitt

Demanding His Secret Son by Louise Fuller

The Sheikh's Secret Baby by Sharon Kendrick

Look out for more stories in the Secret Heirs of Billionaires series coming soon!

Angela Bissell

THE SICILIAN'S SECRET SON

Recycling programs
for this product may
not exist in your area.

ISBN-13: 978-1-335-47818-4

The Sicilian's Secret Son

First North American publication 2019

Printed in U.S.A.

Angela Bissell lives with her husband and one crazy ragdoll cat in the vibrant harborside city of Wellington, New Zealand. In her twenties, with a wad of savings and a few meager possessions, she took off for Europe, backpacking through Egypt, Israel, Turkey and the Greek Islands before finding her way to London, where she settled and worked in a glamorous hotel for several years. Clearly the perfect grounding for her love of Harlequin Presents! Visit her at angelabissell.com.

Books by Angela Bissell

Harlequin Presents

Ruthless Billionaire Brothers

A Night, A Consequence, A Vow
A Mistress, A Scandal, A Ring

Irresistible Mediterranean Tycoons

Surrendering to the Vengeful Italian
Defying Her Billionaire Protector

Visit the Author Profile page
at Harlequin.com for more titles.

CHAPTER ONE

Dino Rossini sat forward, an ugly sneer on his face. 'You're making a mistake, Cavallari. You think this is what your father wanted?'

Seated behind the desk in his late father's study, Luca Cavallari met Rossini's angry stare with a steady one of his own. Glancing away—even blinking— would show weakness, and this man, like all bullies, preyed on those he considered weaker than himself.

It was why Luca had just fired him.

'What my father wanted ceased to matter the day he died,' he said. 'We do things my way now.'

Rossini's expression darkened. 'The old ways—'

'Will not be tolerated. I made that clear two months ago.' A warning his father's security chief had blatantly ignored. Disgust turned Luca's voice rough. 'What you did yesterday was indefensible.'

'He stole from you,' Rossini said, as if that justified his brutality.

'You should have called the police.'

Rossini laughed, the sound harsh. Mean. 'This

isn't New York. You think a fancy suit and haircut gets you respect?' He shook his head. 'America made you soft, Cavallari. Here, when someone steals from you, disrespects you, you don't call the police. You teach him a lesson.'

Anger sent Luca surging to his feet. He leant forward, planting his fisted hands on the desk. 'A *lesson*?' His voice boomed inside the high-ceilinged room. 'You set your men—your thugs—onto a sixteen-year-old boy! He has a fractured leg, broken ribs, a dislocated shoulder and a serious concussion.' Bile burned the back of Luca's throat. Controlling his temper, he sat back down and said coldly, 'Get out.'

'What about my men?'

'They're fired, too.'

Rossini stood, another sneer distorting his face. 'It won't be easy replacing us.'

'I already have.' Luca punctuated the fact with a hard, satisfied smile. 'There are two men outside the door waiting to escort you off the estate.'

Rossini's cheeks turned a deeper shade of mottled red. He strode to the door, shot Luca one last belligerent look, and stalked out.

Luca stood and moved to the window behind the desk. Outside, in the bright glare of the Sicilian sun, two large, muscular men accompanied Rossini to where his black sedan was parked. He got in, gunned the engine and sped off, the car's tyres spitting gravel and kicking up a cloud of pale dust. Luca watched the vehicle vanish from sight.

Good riddance.

He should have fired Rossini two months ago, his twenty years of service to the family be damned. Perhaps the man was right to some extent, although it galled Luca to admit it. He wasn't 'soft'—far from it—but years of self-imposed exile in America had left him ill prepared for the mammoth job ahead.

'Signor Cavallari?'

He turned away from the window to find Victor, the family's long-serving butler and head of the domestic staff, standing in the room.

Luca returned to the chair behind the expansive hand-carved desk—the place from where Franco Cavallari had ruled both his empire and his family with an iron fist—and sat. 'What is it, Victor?' he said, casting his gaze over the endless piles of paperwork demanding his attention.

'I need to show you something.'

The urgency in Victor's voice brought Luca's head up. He studied the man. Not a hair out of place as usual, and his standard pinstriped suit looked as if it had come straight off the housekeeper's steam press. But his brow glistened with beads of sweat and the knuckles on his left hand, which clutched an over-sized envelope against his chest, shone white.

Luca leaned back in his chair. Well, well. Something had got the unflappable Victor in a flap. 'For God's sake, man,' he said. 'Sit down before you fall down.'

Victor dropped into the chair Rossini had vacated.

'Thank you, *signor*.' He plucked a pristine white handkerchief from his breast pocket and dabbed his brow.

Growing impatient, Luca held out his hand.

Victor hesitated, opened his mouth and closed it again, then relinquished the envelope.

Expecting documents of some kind, Luca removed the contents and instead found himself holding a bunch of eight-by-ten colour photographs. He examined the top one. A young woman stood on the grass in what looked like a public park. Other people milled about, but the photographer had clearly focused on her. The weather was sunny and presumably warm since she wore shorts, a sleeveless T-shirt, and a straw sunhat that cast her face in shadow.

'Stunning,' he murmured, trailing an appreciative eye over shapely curves and long, slender legs.

Victor clicked his tongue. 'The other photos,' he urged, pointing at the pile. 'Look at them…the child…'

Luca put the picture down and picked up the next, this one of a young boy playing outdoors. No older than three or four, the child had tousled dark hair, brown eyes fringed with thick lashes, and olive skin flushed with exertion.

The hairs on Luca's forearms lifted.

It was a photo of him as a boy. Except it wasn't, because the date stamp was only ten months old.

What the hell?

He glanced at Victor, who mopped his brow with renewed vigour. 'Where did these come from?'

'Your father's apartment in Rome. I had his things packed and sent here, as Signora Cavallari requested. She asked me to sort through the boxes—'

'She has seen these?'

'Of course not.' Victor's voice held a note of affront. 'I brought them straight to you.'

Good. He wasn't close to his mother, but he had no wish to see her humiliated. It was possible, even likely, that Eva Cavallari knew her husband had kept a mistress—but an illegitimate child? A half-sibling to Luca and his brother Enzo?

He ground his teeth together. Another goddamned mess to clean up, but this went beyond the realm of money laundering and illegal business activities.

This involved a child. A child who could one day stake a legitimate claim for a share of the Cavallari wealth.

Luca flicked through the rest of the photos, found one of the woman without her sunhat, and held it up for a better look.

Blonde and beautiful. Of course. If nothing else, Franco Cavallari had had good taste in women. And she really was exquisite. Startling blue eyes, amazing bone structure, flawless skin...

Luca frowned.

A voice whispered in his head. *You know her.*

No. He shoved the notion away. It was crazy. Fanciful. The world was full of blue-eyed, flaxen-haired beauties. Why would his mind even go there after all these years?

And yet…

He drew the photo closer, trailing his gaze over an elegant cheekbone and down to her pretty mouth.

The camera had caught her at a circumspect moment, and, as such, no smile adorned her face. But Luca realised with sudden, heart-stopping certainty that he already knew this woman's smile. Knew the exact angle at which her lips would tilt, how perfect her teeth would look, and how prominently those incredible cheekbones would stand out. Her blue eyes would sparkle like sunlight on water and when she laughed…

Luca swallowed, his throat gone dry.

When she laughed, it'd be the sweetest, most alluring sound he'd ever heard.

He closed his eyes, his mind catapulting him back to a frigid February night in London. He'd been walking the streets, headed back to his hotel, lost in a dark mire of thought until he'd collided with something soft that bounced off his hard body, reeled backwards, and landed in a clump of dirty snow with a small *oomph*.

Not something but some*one*, he'd realised, staring down at the young woman he'd accidentally bowled off her feet.

She should have yelled at him. Told him to look where he was going. Instead she pushed off her hood, revealing a head of golden hair and a pair of striking blue eyes, and grinned up at him.

Luca had stood dumbstruck for long seconds before he'd finally roused himself, helped her up and found his voice to apologise. And then he'd whisked her into the hotel's swanky lounge bar and ordered her an enormous hot chocolate.

Which was where their random encounter should have ended.

But her natural beauty, her easy smile, her infectious laughter…everything about her captivated him, and the temptation to touch, to hold her close and lose himself in her sweetness—to pretend for one night his world was not tainted with ugliness—was too strong to resist.

Breathing hard, Luca riffled through the photos, searching for something more, some clue, *anything* to help him understand how the woman he'd spent one unforgettable night with five years ago had become not only his father's mistress but the mother of Franco's illegitimate child.

Hatred flared. How typical of his father to corrupt the one pure thing Luca had ever had.

He upended the envelope and a piece of paper, folded in half, fell out. He flipped it open. It was a photocopy of a birth certificate for an Ethan Sinclair, the boy in the photos presumably.

He skipped down to the mother's name.

Annah Sinclair.

And just like that, the memory of her sweet, melodic voice filled his head.

'Annah with an "h",' she'd said, smiling at him over the frothy rim of her hot chocolate.

He'd misunderstood. 'Hannah?'

She'd laughed, shaking her head, then spelt it for him.

Luca thrust aside the memory and focused on the certificate. The father was listed as unknown. The kid's birth date was October the thirty-first in the year—

He froze.

'Signor Cavallari?'

He looked at Victor but didn't see him. In his head, he swiftly calculated the number of months and weeks between February the seventeenth and October the thirty-first.

Victor spoke again, but the sudden rush of blood in Luca's ears and the loud rasp of his breathing drowned out the older man's words.

Wrong.

He had it all wrong.

The boy wasn't Luca's half-brother; he was his *son*.

'Oh, don't you dare,' Annah muttered, throwing down her shears and lunging for the spool of silver ribbon rolling across her worktop.

She was fast, but the renegade ribbon was faster. Before her outstretched fingers could reach it, the reel had gathered momentum and shot off the counter.

Annah groaned, listened to the clatter of the cylinder hitting the floor, and imagined the hideously expensive organza ribbon unravelling beneath her workbench.

Excellent.

She pulled a face at the bunch of purple tulips in her hand. 'Sorry, you lot. I'm afraid you'll have to hang tight.' She set the flowers on the bench and crouched down to search the floor.

No trail of ribbon.

No reel in sight, either.

Puffing a strand of hair out of her face, she got to her hands and knees and crawled beneath her work space.

Please don't let a customer walk in right now.

She loved customers. Who didn't when you ran your own business? But with Chloe—her friend and co-owner of their floral studio—in London visiting a sick friend, Annah was operating alone and stretched to capacity.

She stuck her hand in a gap between some boxes of coloured binding wires stacked against the wall. 'There you are,' she said, closing her fingers around the spool—just as the vintage shopkeeper's bell over the front door of the studio jangled.

Blast.

Hoping to see the scrawny bare legs of her delivery man, she peeped under the front of the counter.

Nope. Not Brian's legs. He didn't wear dark tailored

trousers and expensive-looking leather shoes. Hand-made shoes, by the look of them.

Her walk-in wasn't a local, then. The men who lived in and around the small rural village of Holly-field in South Devon typically wore wellies or work boots, not the kind of shoes that wouldn't survive a muddy field or a half-decent snowfall.

'I'll be right with you,' she called, backing out of the crawl space.

'Please, do not rush on my account,' replied a deep masculine voice.

An accented voice.

Annah stiffened for a second and then, in her haste to stand, misjudged her clearance of the bench. With a loud crack, the top of her skull connected with solid wood. Pain knifed across her scalp. Clutching her head, she dropped back to her knees. 'Ow!'

The man walked around the counter. 'Are you all right?'

His deep voice floated somewhere above her in the flower-scented air.

'Yes,' she lied, not moving, her heart racing in her chest. 'I'm fine.'

You're not fine. You're about to have one of those silly paranoia attacks. After all these years!

Lowering her hands to the floor, she took a deep breath and steadied herself. She mustn't overreact. A man had walked into her shop. He had a sexy Italian accent. Those facts could mean nothing.

Or they could mean—

No.

She shut down the thought and clenched her teeth against the swell of panic. She would not become that woman again. The one who looked over her shoulder and flinched at shadows, seeing threats where none existed. It wasn't fair to Ethan. Her son was an intuitive little boy who deserved better than a nervous wreck for a mother.

'Are you sure?' the man said.

She pushed to her feet. She would look at him and prove she was being ridiculous. With any luck he'd be short and rotund, nothing at all like the tall, dark-haired devil who'd seduced her with hot chocolate and a hint of torment in his deep brown eyes on a cold night in London five years before.

More importantly, he'd be nothing like Ethan's paternal grandfather—a man she hoped never to have the misfortune of meeting again.

'Yes, thank you,' she said, placing the reel of ribbon on the counter. The top of her head throbbed, but she turned towards the man with a professional smile. He was probably passing through and had stopped to buy flowers for his girlfriend or wife. 'How can I help?'

The lapels of a sleek, single-breasted camel coat worn over a black polo-neck jumper confronted her at eye level, along with a set of extremely broad shoulders. Although Annah couldn't see the body beneath the coat, her immediate impression was of solidity and power.

Her smile faltered, and, in the same way people peek through their fingers at a scary movie, afraid to look yet helplessly compelled to do so, she lifted her gaze.

A pair of dark brown eyes, deep-set in a brutally handsome face, connected with hers.

'Hello, Annah.'

She gasped, her heart lunging into her throat, and stumbled backwards, colliding with the workbench.

Luca Cavallari moved towards her. 'Careful—'

'Don't touch me,' she blurted, and grabbed the first object to hand—her florist shears—and stuck them out in front of her.

He looked down at the small pair of secateurs and then back at her, his expression more quizzical than alarmed. He spoke softly. 'You would stab me, Annah?'

'Maybe.' She firmed her grip on the shears. Of course she wouldn't stab him, but he didn't know that. He didn't know *her*. They were strangers, regardless of the fact that they'd created an amazing little person together.

Anyway, people were capable of all sorts of things when something dear to them was threatened. Annah would do anything to protect her son, especially from the people who'd wanted him gone long before he'd drawn his first breath.

The bell over the door tinkled and Annah glanced towards the entrance. *Mistake*, she realised as Luca Cavallari seized her wrist and deftly disarmed her, tossing the shears down the far end of the bench beyond her reach. 'No!' she cried, tugging her wrist, but his one-handed grip was too strong.

Annah cast a panicky look at the newcomer—a thick-necked behemoth dressed in black—and her stomach plummeted. She glared at Luca with false bravado. 'Really? You brought reinforcements?'

He frowned as if her hostility perplexed him, and that incensed her. What had he expected? Not a warm reception, surely. If only she'd had the presence of mind to act as if she didn't recognise him. She'd spent one night with him five years ago; it was entirely plausible that his face had faded from her memory.

Except the truth was it hadn't.

How could she forget the man she'd recklessly given her virginity to—the only man she'd ever slept with—when every day she looked at a tiny, living replica of him?

Thoughts of Ethan spiked her anxiety. Her one chance to play it cool was gone. She'd overreacted. Tipped her hand by revealing her fear. If he hadn't already known she had something to hide, he knew now.

She looked at the man in black, her heart beating so hard her chest hurt, then back to Luca, whose eyes narrowed as he scrutinised her face.

His frown deepened. He switched his gaze to the other man and said something in Italian. Immediately, the man exited the studio and crossed the street to a big black SUV parked up by the village shop, two wheels perched on the footpath so it didn't block the narrow road.

The shop owner was nowhere in sight, and Annah felt a glimmer of relief. She liked Dorothy Green. The fifty-something widow was kind and well meaning, but she was also incurably nosy. Little happened in Hollyfield without Dot knowing, and new faces always garnered special attention.

'You have nothing to fear,' Luca said in that crushed-velvet voice she knew better than to trust. 'I simply wish to talk.'

And yet he still held her wrist as if he didn't trust her not to reach for a sharp object again. Annah put her shoulders back, pretending her skin wasn't tingling where he touched her and her hormones weren't leaping with awareness of those chiselled good looks and thick-lashed, espresso-coloured eyes.

Setting her jaw, she made herself recall his father's callous treatment of her. His cold dismissal of the child who at the time had been little more than a lentil-sized embryo in her womb, but his grandchild nevertheless!

Where had Luca been then, when *she* wanted to talk? Conveniently absent. In the arms of another woman for all Annah knew, his memory of her already gathering dust while she came to terms with a far more permanent reminder of their night together. Of the one time in her life she'd chosen desire and spontaneity over the inclination to be sensible.

'Talk about what?' she said, clinging to the possibility, remote as it was, that his walking into her floral studio in the middle of the Devon countryside was just a crazy coincidence and he knew nothing of Ethan's existence.

A flimsy hope at best, and Luca crushed it with two words.

'Our son.'

His gaze challenged her to look him in the eye and deny it.

'*My* son,' she said, more ferociously than she'd intended. But he didn't get to show up on her doorstep after four years and pretend he was interested in the son he hadn't wanted. She tugged her wrist again. 'Let me go.'

He released her, and she clasped her arms around her middle, a thousand questions hammering her brain. How and when had he found out she'd gone through with the pregnancy? Why show up now? More specifically, what did he want?

Not Ethan. Please, not Ethan.

She didn't want her little boy anywhere near his paternal family!

By all accounts, Ethan's grandfather was little better than a modern-day gangster. Admittedly, those accounts were based on rumour and originated from an Italian chef with a flair for dramatics whom Chloe had briefly dated in London. But Annah hadn't needed much convincing. She'd met Franco Cavallari, and he'd terrified the living daylights out of her. She'd never met anyone more formidable or intimidating—or so devoid of compassion.

'Annah—'

She held up a hand, closing her eyes, light-headed all of a sudden. 'I… I just need a moment,' she said, because the conversation they were about to have was one she'd believed would never happen. Which meant that she, the woman Chloe had dubbed the Queen of Preparedness, was woefully *ill* prepared.

She opened her eyes and mentally braced for the visual impact of him. Predictably, her pulse spiked at the sight of all that dark, chiselled masculinity. But at least he wasn't touching her now, inflaming the nerves in her wrist and making her body tingle in very inappropriate places.

She did *not* want to feel sexually attracted to this man.

'Are you all right?' he said suddenly. 'Your head. Perhaps it should be checked?'

He shifted towards her, lifting his hands, and she instinctively shrank back. Having Luca Cavallari run his fingers over her scalp would undo her completely.

'My head's fine,' she said hurriedly. 'I'm just a little…overwhelmed. I never imagined having this conversation, to be honest.'

His eyes narrowed. 'You never imagined I would one day wish to know my son?'

Annah didn't like how that question made her insides twist, as if *she* had some reason to feel guilty.

It made her want to push back. 'You haven't met my son. What makes you so certain he's yours?'

'I've seen his birth certificate. And photos.'

Annah blinked. Photos of Ethan? How? She was always so careful. She only used social media for business and she never posted photos of her or Ethan online.

Luca slid his hands into the pockets of his expensive-looking coat. With his dark looks, his lean, broad-shouldered physique and his stylish attire, he wouldn't have looked out of place on a catwalk in Paris or Milan. In Hollyfield, he looked about as alien as Annah had felt the first time she and Chloe had driven into the quaint country village.

'Your son was born at the Royal Devon and Exeter Hospital exactly thirty-six weeks and five days after you and I spent a night together in London,' he said. 'I'm no expert on pregnancy, but I can do the math. Unless you slept with another man around the same time who looks remarkably like me, or you were already pregnant by immaculate conception when we met…' he paused just long enough for Annah's face to flame at his reference to how innocent she'd been '…I am reasonably confident without the aid of a DNA test—which I'm not ruling out, by the way—that Ethan Sinclair is not only your son but *my* son, as well.'

She glared at him, hating that she had no comeback to any of that. 'What photos?' she said instead.

He hesitated for a beat. 'Surveillance photos.'

Annah sucked in a breath. 'You've been having us watched?' Her voice rose in horror. Did he have photos of her, too? The sense of violation made her stomach roil.

'Not me.'

'Then who?' she demanded.

His jaw hardened. 'My father.'

A chill ran up her spine. 'Why?'

'I don't know,' he said tightly.

She shook her head, confused. 'Haven't you asked him?'

'No,' he said.

'Why not?'

'Because he's dead.'

CHAPTER TWO

Luca wondered what, if anything, it said about him that he could announce his father was dead and feel nothing but loathing for the man.

Annah's blue eyes widened, but she didn't offer any trite words of condolence, and her silence strengthened Luca's suspicions that his father had done a damn sight more than place her and their son under surveillance.

At some point she and his father had met. Luca didn't know when or why, but Franco had clearly put the fear of God in her. Why else had her reaction to seeing Luca been to draw a weapon? That the sight of him could provoke fear and panic in anyone, let alone in this woman—the mother of his child—made him feel physically ill.

It'd taken his investigator three days to locate her, during which time he'd gradually come to terms with the knowledge—or the ninety-nine percent certainty at least—that he'd fathered a son.

Travelling by private jet from Palermo to Exeter,

and then by road to this deathly quiet English backwater, had given him time to mentally prepare as much as he could for something so far outside his realm of experience.

It was a luxury he had denied Annah by turning up here unannounced, so he'd expected shock and even defensiveness and guilt, given she'd raised his son without his knowledge for the last four years.

But abject fear?

Even his touch, meant only to calm and gently restrain after disarming her, had induced a wild, trapped look in her eyes. And at the first mention of their son she had turned fierce and possessive, like a tigress protecting her cub. Protecting *his* cub.

For some reason he'd found that inordinately sexy.

The bell over the door jingled and, just like when he'd arrived and again when his man had come and gone, the sound evoked memories of the old-fashioned ice-cream parlour he and his brother had frequented in a small fishing village near their childhood home.

As did anything relating to his brother, the memories stirred a sense of disquietude, and he cast them aside and looked towards the entrance, hoping his bodyguard had not returned. Mario's muscle-bound physique intimidated most people, men included, and Luca had noted how Annah's fear had escalated in response to the big man. Luca had told him to go back to the vehicle and stay there. Mario's job was to put himself between Luca and danger, but Annah was no more a physical threat to Luca than he was to her.

However, it wasn't Mario but a wiry, bald-headed man who entered the shop and crossed to the counter.

Annah turned to him, subtly putting distance between her and Luca. 'Hi, Brian. I'm so sorry but I'm running behind. If you can wait I'll have it ready in a couple of minutes.'

'No problem, see to your customer first,' he said, acknowledging Luca with a courteous nod.

Annah shook her head. 'I'll do Caroline's now. She wants the bouquet for a client meeting at three.' She sent Luca a stiff smile. 'I'm sorry. Perhaps you could come back in ten minutes?'

Luca gave her a look. She would not get rid of him that easily. 'I can wait.'

'Great,' said Brian. 'I'll just pop over to Dot's. Back in a tick.'

The solid workbench behind Annah stretched along the wall at a right angle to the counter. Luca chose a spot at the end, leaned his hips back against the wooden edge, and crossed his arms over his chest.

Annah jammed her hands on her hips and narrowed her eyes at him.

He stared back. 'You and I *are* going to have a conversation.'

'Fine,' she said in a tone that told him it wasn't. She pointed to a spot behind him. 'I need my shears.'

Luca glanced over his shoulder at the 'weapon'

he'd wrested from her earlier. He picked up the shears and held them out, one eyebrow raised. 'Can I trust you with these?'

She gave him a withering look and snatched them out of his hand, then set to work, her nimble fingers moving quickly as she snipped and pruned.

He looked around. The shop wasn't large but the space was well utilised, the décor stylish and contemporary. An elegant logo stencilled on the large front window read 'Scent Floral Boutique'. His investigator's report had revealed that Annah co-owned this business. Luca recalled her talking that night in London about her ambition to open a floral studio with her friend.

'Congratulations on the business,' he said.

She paused her work and stared at him.

He added, 'It was your goal, was it not?'

After a moment's hesitation, she said, 'Yes. It was.'

'You should be proud.' As soon as he said it he realised the words sounded patronising. It wasn't how he'd meant them. He knew well the challenge of building a business from the ground up. He'd built a successful private equity firm in New York. It had taken five years of relentless work, but he didn't regret a single minute. There was something deeply satisfying about earning a legitimate living—a concept his father had never embraced despite Luca's attempts to steer him down a respectable path.

A village floristry shop and a billion-dollar investment firm were light years apart on the business spectrum, but the over-arching principles for success were the same.

And Annah wasn't only running a business, she was raising a child.

His child.

A responsibility she shouldn't have to shoulder alone—and wouldn't have to from now on.

She resumed her work. Luca pulled out his phone. If he didn't occupy himself he would stand there watching her and his mind would end up going where it shouldn't. As it was he had noticed too much. Her exquisite bone structure; her flawless complexion; her slim yet curvaceous figure. Her eyes were still that startling shade of blue, her long hair still golden and glossy.

Five years ago, he wouldn't have believed Annah Sinclair could grow more beautiful. But she had.

Frowning, Luca stared at his phone and concentrated on his email until Brian returned. Annah handed him the large bouquet she'd skilfully fashioned out of the flowers and greenery on her workbench and, after Brian had left, locked the door and flipped an open/closed sign on the glass to 'Closed'. She strode to the rear of the shop, untying and removing her red apron as she went, leaving a plain outfit of slim-fitting black trousers and a long-sleeved white top.

She hung the apron on a hook. 'I can give you half an hour, but then I need to pick up my son.'

He put his phone in his pocket. 'From where?'

'Nursery.' She turned. 'We can talk up here,' she said over her shoulder, and started up a flight of stairs.

Luca followed. The stairwell was narrow and the steep stairs creaked under his weight. He concentrated on where he put his feet rather than looking at Annah's backside swaying above him. At the top she paused on a small landing, opened a door, and led him into a large room.

A rush of warmth and sunlight greeted him. He looked around. The long open-plan space incorporated lounge and dining areas and a small kitchen with a breakfast bar.

The investigator's report had listed the same physical address for Annah's home and business, and suddenly Luca realised he was standing in his son's home, on a rug that Ethan had probably walked and crawled across a thousand times.

A strange sensation tugged at Luca's gut. He surveyed the room again, this time noticing a box filled with toys next to the sofa, a blue and white plastic truck under the coffee table, and a cat—a real cat with ginger fur—curled up on an armchair. A large framed photo of Annah and Ethan hung on the wall. Mother and child both grinned into the camera lens. It was a beautiful photo.

Luca dragged his gaze from it. 'How long have you lived here?'

'Since before Ethan was born.'

He glanced back towards the stairs and tried to imagine tackling them with an armful of shopping bags, or a stroller and a baby or toddler in tow.

Annah closed the door. 'I'll put the kettle on and make some tea.'

Ah, yes. The quintessentially English answer to every problem. A cup of tea. Luca would have welcomed an espresso or even a shot of whiskey, but if the ritual of making tea settled Annah's nerves and eased the way for a difficult conversation, he'd happily drink a gallon of the stuff.

Annah went to the kitchen, and Luca crossed to a window overlooking the back of the property. Outside the kitchen was a roof terrace with a small wrought-iron table, two chairs, and a bunch of potted plants. The terrace was accessible from both the kitchen and a set of external steps leading down to a courtyard, where a dark blue hatchback was parked. A narrow driveway snaked around the side of the building and a brick wall separated the rear of the property from dense woodland.

From a safety perspective, Luca was glad the upstairs flat had another route of access. But he couldn't help surveying the concrete courtyard and the tiny terrace and comparing them to the outdoor space he and Enzo had enjoyed growing up, including landscaped gardens, citrus and olive groves, and even a vineyard.

A fierce desire rose in him for his son to experience that, too. To have the freedom to run and play and explore the land that would one day be his. Land that Luca had thought was lost to him, along with everything else associated with the Cavallari legacy, until recently. Now he had the opportunity to shape that legacy in the way *he* saw fit. To take what Franco Cavallari had sullied and turn it into something good. Something worth passing on to the next generation.

Hearing the electric kettle turn off, he glanced towards the kitchen. Annah stood on the other side of the breakfast bar, her back to him. He wandered over. A teapot sat on the bench, lid off, waiting to be filled.

She stood motionless.

'Annah?'

She swung around and looked at him. 'You could leave.'

He frowned. 'Excuse me?'

'You could just go,' she said, stepping closer, eyes wide as she looked up at him, 'and we could both pretend you were never here. You'll never hear from us—I promise. I'll never contact you. Never ask for money. Never ask you for anything *ever*.'

Anger flickered. She thought he was the kind of man who could walk away and pretend his son—his own flesh and blood—didn't exist?

He clenched his jaw. 'Make the tea, Annah.'

'Luca…' She spoke his name like a husky entreaty, and it reached inside him, evoking a memory as scorchingly vivid as if she'd lain beneath him only yesterday, driving him to the brink with her soft, seductive pleas.

Don't stop, Luca. Please…don't stop.

He nearly had. When her body's tight resistance and her stifled cry of pain had given rise to a shocking realisation, Luca had frozen mid-thrust, then almost reflexively withdrawn. But it was too late by then. He couldn't *un*breach her innocence. He was deep inside her and she was clinging like a limpet, stubbornly—and sexily—refusing to let him go.

Thrusting the memory aside, Luca unbuttoned his coat, took it off, and draped it over the back of a dining chair. 'Black,' he said, sliding his hands into his trouser pockets. 'No sugar. And I'll have it strong, thanks.'

Annah blinked, and the pleading look vanished from her eyes. She finished making the tea in silence. Only once they were seated at the small dining table, steaming mugs in front of them, did she speak again. 'When did your father die?' she asked quietly.

'Two months ago.'

She nodded slowly. Her hands were wrapped around her mug, and she stared into her tea for so long his patience began to unravel.

'Are you going to tell me what happened, Annah, or will I have to drag it out of you?'

Her gaze snapped up. 'It's obvious what happened, isn't it? I didn't do what you wanted.'

He frowned. 'I don't know what that means.'

'Oh, come on, Luca.' The way she said his name this time wasn't husky; it was hard and bitter, saturated with scepticism. 'You might not have had the nerve to try paying me off in person, but your father made it clear he was representing your interests.'

Dread knotted Luca's stomach. He needed the truth, but at the same time he wanted to close his ears, sensing that whatever was coming would destroy any lingering shred of the love he'd once felt for his father.

'When?' he said.

Annah's eyebrows knitted. 'I'm sorry?'

'When did you speak to my father?'

'Why are you asking—?'

'Please, Annah,' he cut in. 'Just tell me.'

She pulled her hands away from her mug, sat back and clasped her arms around her middle. 'Late March. In London. At the Cavallari offices.'

Luca's lungs locked as if someone had sucker-punched him in the chest.

Annah frowned. 'What?'

He took a moment to collect his thoughts, get the air moving in his lungs again. 'Do you remember what I told you that night in London? About leaving for the States the next day?'

'Yes. You'd left your job. You were moving to New York the next day.'

As much as he had wanted her that night, his conscience had forbidden him to seduce her with false promises. His flight to New York had already been booked. There had been nothing left for him in Europe. In Sicily. His father had declared him an outcast, made it brutally clear that Luca would never be welcomed back. He'd been upfront with Annah about his impending departure. One night of pleasure was all he offered. Nothing more.

He pushed his tea aside and sat forward. 'Three days before you and I met, my father and I had a falling-out. The job I'd left was my position in the London office of Cavallari Enterprises.' He'd vacated both his office and the company apartment on the same day, checking into a hotel and taking only his personal effects with him. He hadn't wanted anything that was paid for with Franco Cavallari's ill-gotten gains. 'After I left, I had no contact whatsoever with anyone in the company, my father included.'

Annah stared at him. 'What are you saying?'

'My father and I never spoke again. The next time I saw him, he was lying in a casket.' Luca paused, giving her a minute to process his words. 'What did you mean about a pay-off? A pay-off for what?'

Annah hesitated, her eyes wide. 'An abortion,' she whispered.

Annah and Luca stared at each other across the table.

'Tell me everything,' he said, his expression grim.

She sucked in her breath, her mind grappling with the implications of what he'd told her. If it was true, everything she'd believed about him in the last five years was wrong.

'Start at the beginning,' he said, his tone gentling

as if he realised just how deeply he'd shocked her. 'When did you discover you were pregnant?'

'Four weeks later.' Her voice was not as steady as she hoped. 'It didn't occur to me before then that I might be pregnant. I mean…we used protection.'

Her face heated and she glanced away. She didn't want to think about sex with Luca. Not while he was sitting at her dining table looking so handsome and compelling.

Bringing him up here had been a calculated risk. They could have gone to the cosy café at the Wilkinsons' farm shop half a mile down the road, or even sat on a bench in the local park to talk. But they wouldn't have had complete privacy like they had here.

And she wasn't concerned for her safety. Despite her knee-jerk reaction downstairs, her gut told her Luca wasn't a physical threat to her or Ethan.

'But you weren't on the Pill?'

'No,' Annah confirmed.

'And condoms aren't foolproof,' he added, voicing all the same thoughts that'd run through Annah's head in the beginning, when she'd struggled to accept she was pregnant.

'Apparently not.' She took another deep breath. 'You were entitled to know and I wanted to tell you—but I had no idea how to contact you.' That last sentence sounded faintly accusatory, and she cringed inwardly. She didn't want to sound petulant because he hadn't given her his number. He'd told her he was leaving the country. Annah had understood what he was offering: one night, no strings attached.

Luca brushed a hand over his face, dragging his thumb and fingers down the sides of his jaw. He was clean-shaven, but his five o'clock shadow was already growing in. Annah could hear the scrape of fine stubble under his hand. 'I hadn't thought about the need for contact in case there were…consequences,' he said, his expression pained.

They were both silent.

After a moment, he said, 'Tell me how—and why—you ended up meeting with my father.'

Annah picked up her mug and swallowed a mouthful of tea, then kept the mug in her lap, hands wrapped around it, trying to absorb the lukewarm heat from the china. 'Does it matter now?' she said, her chest tightening at the prospect of reliving the encounter. 'What's done is done. The last five years can't be reversed.'

'It matters,' said Luca, the sudden obdurate angle of his jaw not unlike Ethan's whenever he dug his little heels in about something.

Annah sighed. 'I tried to find you on social media,' she said, omitting to mention she'd actually searched the more popular sites *before* discovering she was pregnant. After their night together, forgetting about him had been difficult. Eventually, curiosity had won out, although it didn't get her far. She knew his name but not much else, and she quickly discovered dozens of online profiles for men named

Luca Cavallari. Not one of them was the dark, sexy stranger she'd spent a night with in a plush hotel room in London.

'I'm not on social media.'

'So I discovered.' She put her half-drunk tea on the table. 'I searched the Internet using your name combined with New York and then Rome, since that's where you said you were originally from.' But that had been a lie; Luca was Sicilian. 'It took ages, but eventually I came across a photo of you at a gala fundraiser in Rome.'

Annah's heart had leapt at the two-dimensional image of him, gorgeous and suave in a tuxedo, then plunged when she'd seen the glamorous woman on his arm. The photo had been two years old at the time, but her stomach had still twisted with silly jealousy. 'The caption mentioned your family's company. I discovered there was an office in London and called to see if someone could give me a phone number or email address for you.

'I got the runaround, though. The receptionist said you'd left and they didn't have forwarding details. I couldn't believe that no one in your own family's company was able to contact you. I kept calling back, but I just got transferred to a different person with the same story.'

It had been so frustrating—and humiliating. 'In the end I lost my cool and did something stupid,' she confessed. 'I blurted out that I was pregnant with your child and suggested somebody might like to pass on the information.' She huffed out a humourless laugh. 'It got a reaction at least. A woman called me within an hour and invited me to go in for a meeting two days later.'

Annah looked down at her hands. 'Until I got there, I'd thought maybe I was going to meet you,' she said, stopping short of confessing that a part of her had fizzed with anticipation at the prospect despite the awkward circumstances. 'But it was your father.'

She glanced at Luca. A deep groove had settled between his eyebrows, and a muscle flickered in his jaw.

'He wasn't very kind,' she said, vastly understating Franco Cavallari's demeanour. 'He treated me like a gold digger. Wrote a cheque for ten thousand pounds and told me to go have an abortion.' Her voice wobbled at the memory. 'I tried to leave without taking it, but he pushed it into my bag and then had me escorted out of the building. I ripped the cheque up as soon as I got home,' she added.

'What else did he say?'

'Not much.'

'Annah.'

She sighed again. 'He said you would have handled it yourself if you were still in the country. Then he said you wished me well and hoped this would put an end to the matter.'

Those words had cut deeper than any others. After a burly man had shown her the door, she'd hurried away on shaky legs, found a toilet in a shopping mall and promptly thrown up.

'Did he threaten you?'

'Not exactly—not in words. But he was…intimidating.' And convincing. Annah had gone home believing the worst—that Luca had spurned her and his unborn child and not had the courage or decency to do it in person.

Emotion clogged her throat, and she rose suddenly and rushed to the back door. With trembling hands she tried to open it, but the deadbolt jammed and she cursed under her breath—why hadn't the landlord replaced it like he'd promised?—and then her fingers blurred alarmingly before her eyes.

She blinked furiously. She was not going to cry. She just needed some air.

If only this blasted lock—

It gave way and she yanked the door open, stumbled out to the terrace, and gulped in a breath of the crisp March air. Seconds later the back of her neck tingled, alerting her to Luca's presence before his deep voice rumbled behind her.

'I didn't know you were pregnant, Annah. If I had, all this would have turned out very differently. It's important you understand that as we move forward.'

Move forward?

Annah wasn't sure she wanted to know what that entailed.

Curling her hands over the railing, she looked out at the treetops and the hilly fields and farmland beyond.

It was quiet in Hollyfield—too quiet sometimes—but the countryside was pretty, the area safe, the villagers friendly and kind.

She and Ethan were settled here. Content. She didn't want his life disrupted like hers had been too often as a child.

But Luca was here and he wasn't going away. Annah had to deal with this. Deal with him. Straightening her back, she turned and faced him. 'What now?'

'Take me to my son,' he said.

CHAPTER THREE

Luca returned to the SUV, got in the back, and instructed Mario to follow Annah's hatchback. Apparently, his son's daycare facility was in a neighbouring village, about a fifteen-minute drive away, according to Annah.

She hadn't looked thrilled about taking him to meet his son, but her grudging acquiescence was a win nonetheless. Still, Luca didn't count on plain sailing ahead. Annah Sinclair was no pushover; she was a tougher version of the woman he'd met five years ago, and a damn sight less trusting.

He fisted his hand on his thigh. If his father wasn't already dead he'd wring the bastard's neck.

Listening to Annah's account of what had happened, Luca had felt winded and then furious at what Franco had done.

Had his father hated him that much?

Bile burned the back of Luca's throat. The answers to so many questions had gone with Franco Cavallari to his grave—including why he'd had photos of Annah and Ethan in his possession, and, more disturbingly, what he'd planned to do with them.

For the next ten minutes Mario sat on the tail of the hatchback. Annah drove at a fair clip, obviously familiar with the winding back roads and country lanes. When they reached the village she parked on a side road and Mario pulled up behind her.

She got out, crossed the road, and disappeared through a gate in a high wooden fence.

A full minute passed with no sign of her, then another. Luca tapped his fingers against his thigh.

How long did it take to collect a child?

He watched other vehicles come and go. Other parents disappear through the gate, all of whom emerged soon after with one or more children in tow.

He got out of the SUV and paced the footpath, stopping every few seconds to glare across the road. From behind the wheel, Mario sent him a look that was vaguely amused, and Luca gave him a dark scowl.

He looked across the road again. Perhaps he should go in?

No sooner had the thought formed than the gate swung open, and Annah came out holding the hand of a dark-haired boy.

Luca froze. Suddenly, his heartbeat sped up and his hands went clammy.

He was about to meet his child. An event for which he had no point of reference. No previous experience to help him navigate this unfamiliar territory.

He stared at Ethan, so like himself as a boy, and a memory surfaced. A vignette of the Cavallari family in happier times, years before ugly revelations had torn them apart and planted them on opposite sides of an unbridgeable divide.

The day was hot and they were picnicking on the family estate. Luca was young, no older than Ethan, and he was riding high on his *papà*'s shoulders, giggling and shrieking as Franco put his arms out like an airplane and raced across the lawn. His mother wore a pretty sundress and sat under a big oak, baby Enzo cradled in her arms. Luca could hear the sweet tinkle of her laughter, unaware that in years to come he would rarely hear his mother laugh.

Luca had loved his father. It pained him to admit it, but he had. He'd idolised him. Wanted to be him. In the eyes of his young son, Franco Cavallari had been an important man. Wealthy and successful. Handsome and charismatic. Other men treated him with deference—and respect.

Luca had been a teenager when he'd finally understood it wasn't respect his father engendered in other men, but fear.

On the night Franco initiated his eldest son into manhood, Luca's love for him had turned into something confusing and complex. A gut-churning mix of revulsion and love and hatred he struggled for years to understand.

His first big mistake was believing he could change his father. His second was not destroying Franco when he had the chance. Emotion had made him weak. Incapable of doing what had to be done.

If he had been stronger, if he'd taken Franco down, he could have saved his brother.

He took a deep breath and calmed his heart rate. He wouldn't fail Ethan like he had failed Enzo. He could do this. He was a better man than Franco; he could be a better father. All he had to do was stay focused and control his emotions.

'Is that him, Mummy?'

Ethan tugged on Annah's hand. Standing with her feet glued to the pavement, she swallowed down a bubble of nervous laughter. 'Yes, sweetheart,' she said, staring across the road. 'That's him.'

'Holy Moly,' breathed a woman's voice.

Annah glanced to her left. Harriet, a frazzled but good-humoured mother of five, stood with her youngest—a little girl with ginger ringlets—balanced on her hip.

Harriet, like Ethan, stared across the road. So did several other mothers as they trotted along the street and bundled their kids into cars. Annah couldn't blame them. Luca Cavallari was a knee-weakening mix of smouldering sex appeal and unadulterated machismo.

'Who is *that*?' said Harriet.

Ethan leaned around Annah's legs. 'That's my daddy,' he said proudly.

Oh, God. The footpath swayed beneath Annah's feet. She closed her eyes for a moment. When she opened them, Harriet was looking at her, bug-eyed.

'Wow,' said Harriet. 'That's…unexpected?'

This time she couldn't stop the nervous laughter escaping. 'You could say that.'

Harriet put a hand on Annah's arm and squeezed gently. 'Let me know if you need anything, hon.'

Annah managed a smile. 'Thanks.'

Harriet headed off to her car, and Annah looked across the road again. Luca wasn't even looking at her. His gaze was fixated on Ethan.

'Mummy?'

'Yes?'

'You're holding on too tight.'

'Oh!' Annah loosened her grip on Ethan's hand and looked into his upturned face. 'Sorry, sweetheart.' She smiled, hoping it looked less strained than it felt, and he beamed back.

'Are we crossing now?'

His little voice rang with eagerness, and Annah's heart clenched. Ethan was excited to meet his father, but she was still grappling with shock and anxiety. She would have appreciated a few days' grace—time to get her emotions under control before introducing Ethan to his father—but Luca had different ideas.

Annah had tried to put herself in his shoes. He had missed out on the first four years of his son's life. Wanting to meet his child without further delay perhaps wasn't unreasonable.

Reminding Ethan to look both ways for traffic, she crossed the road with him. Luca waited on the other side. He wasn't wearing his coat, and his all-black attire combined with his sheer size and the intense expression he wore made him look rather intimidating. But as they drew close he squatted down, bringing his face level with Ethan's, a smile curving his lips that not only softened his hard features but caused Annah's pulse to hitch.

'Hello, Ethan,' he said. 'My name is Luca.'

Ethan blinked and then looked to Annah, shyness overtaking him now that he was face to face with the commanding figure of his father.

Annah smiled reassuringly. 'It's okay, sweetheart. Say hello.'

He turned back to Luca. 'Hello.' His hand reached out and touched Luca's bent knee, as though to make sure he was real. He pulled his hand back, broke into a grin, and boldly announced, 'You're my daddy.'

Luca shot Annah a surprised look.

She lifted one shoulder. 'I thought honesty was best.' She could have made something up. Introduced Luca as her 'friend'. But then what? Ethan would learn the truth eventually, and then he'd know she'd lied to him.

Their eyes held for a moment.

'Thank you,' he said quietly.

Annah gave a single small nod, his gratitude

sparking a warm glow she hadn't expected—and wasn't sure she should welcome. Not when she and Luca could be headed for opposite sides of a custody battle.

His attention returned to Ethan. 'I am,' he said. 'Although where I come from we say *papà*.'

'Where are you from?' Ethan asked, and Annah suddenly realised she had no idea how far Luca had travelled to get here or where he lived these days. New York? London? Sicily? Rome?

Her stomach tightened. How would a shared custody arrangement work if she and Luca lived in different countries?

'A long way away,' Luca said.

'Is that why you haven't come to see me before?'

Annah winced inwardly. Seeing the discomfort on Luca's face, she stepped in to rescue him. 'Come on, sweetheart. The ducks will be wondering where we are.'

Ethan turned back to his father. 'Are you coming to feed the ducks?'

Annah held her breath. In his handmade Italian shoes and tailored trousers, Luca wasn't exactly dressed for a walk in the reserve, but she'd thrown the invitation out there anyway. This was part of her and Ethan's weekly routine; Luca could fit in or not.

'Yes.' He straightened up. 'Your mother invited me. Is that all right with you?'

Ethan clapped his hands. 'Yes!'

Annah forced herself to smile. It was stupid, but

Ethan's enthusiasm towards his father felt like a kick in her ribs. 'Come on, then,' she said, imbuing her voice with a cheerfulness she didn't feel. 'Let's go before it gets too cold.'

Half an hour later, Annah sat on a bench seat carved out of an old gnarled tree trunk and hunched her shoulders inside her jacket.

It wasn't all that cold. This part of the nature reserve was sheltered from the cool breeze, and the early spring sunshine lent a modicum of warmth to the afternoon.

The chill was inside her. A cold knot of anxiety that wasn't going to shift any time soon, at least not until she knew what Luca's long-term intentions were.

She watched him and Ethan at the water's edge, scooping handfuls of oats, seeds and food pellets out of a paper bag and tossing them into the midst of a noisy gathering of ducks. Farther out, a pair of white swans glided across the calm surface of the landscaped lake.

It was a pretty spot and one of her and Ethan's favourite haunts. Throughout the reserve, wild daffodils already bloomed in bright patches of cheerful yellow. In another few weeks, spring would start throwing its confetti of colour across the countryside in earnest. The wedding season would gear up, and work would get busy. Annah and Chloe had made a name for themselves specialising in wedding flowers and event styling. Last year they'd even won an award for South West Wedding Florist of the Year.

She wished Chloe were here now. She wasn't only Annah's business partner, she was her best friend. Her only close friend really. Annah knew plenty of people, was friendly with most, but she struggled to make that leap from acquaintance to friend. Learning to rely on herself as a child had made her fiercely independent, inclined to put walls up when she didn't necessarily mean to.

But walls could be good. Especially if you didn't know who to trust.

Could she trust Luca?

According to Chloe's ex, Franco Cavallari had been a corrupt and powerful businessman with ties to organised crime. Just because Luca had fallen out with his father, it didn't mean he wasn't a bad guy, too.

And bad guys didn't mind doing bad things, did they? Things like…kidnap their own children?

Oh, Lord.

Annah jammed the brakes on her imagination. Luca's behaviour so far had been perfectly civilised, she reminded herself. He'd sat down and had a cup of tea with her, for goodness' sake!

And now he stood on a muddy lakeside feeding a bunch of ducks with Ethan. It almost made her smile. She'd bet his fancy leather shoes were toast.

'All gone, Mummy,' Ethan called to her, tipping

the paper bag upside down to show it was empty. 'Can we go see Sandy now?'

'Yes.' Annah stood and pushed a smile onto her face as Ethan and Luca came towards her. Seeing them together like this, side by side, made her jumbled emotions even more difficult to untangle. The physical similarities—dark hair, brown eyes, olive skin—brought a lump to her throat.

Shoving the empty paper bag at Annah, Ethan said to his father, 'Sandy's got eight babies!'

Luca returned a suitable look of surprise. 'Eight?' he said, raising a quizzical eyebrow at Annah.

'Puppies,' she clarified. 'Sandy's a golden retriever. She belongs to the family who runs the café and lives in the house up by the entrance.'

'They were too small to hold last time but they might be big enough now,' Ethan chipped in, then chattered excitedly all the way to the café, something like awe lighting up his face every time he tipped his head back to gaze up at his father.

As they stepped into the warmth of the café, Annah wrestled down a pang of jealousy. She didn't need to compete for Ethan's affections. He loved her. She was his mummy. Luca's sudden arrival didn't change that.

Going straight to the window table where she and Ethan usually sat, she unzipped her puffer jacket and then hung it on the back of a chair. Not until she glanced up did she notice Luca's burly associate sitting at a table in a back corner.

He got to his feet, and Annah's pulse did a nervous skitter. While he wasn't the same man who had wrapped a bruising hand around her arm five years ago and 'escorted' her from the Cavallari Enterprises offices after Luca's father had carelessly dismissed her, the likeness was enough to make the hairs on the back of her neck lift.

Instinctively, without taking her eyes off the man, she reached for Ethan and dragged him close.

Luca narrowed his gaze on Annah's face and watched her complexion go from peaches and cream to chalky white. Her hands clutched Ethan's shoulders and she stared at Mario as if expecting him to try to snatch up her child and steal him away.

Gripped by an urge to reassure, Luca set his hand against the small of her back and felt her flinch. She darted him a look that made his stomach harden. There was no weapon in her hand now, but the wariness and distrust in her eyes told him she was still afraid.

How many times in the months since he'd returned to Sicily had he seen that same expression of trepidation and fear?

Too many.

His father's legacy had tainted the Cavallari name, and many people assumed Luca was cut from the same cloth. Changing that perception and rebuilding trust was proving a slow process.

Luca motioned Mario over. 'Annah, this is Mario

Russo, my driver,' he said. 'Mario, this is Annah Sinclair. And this…' he placed his hand on Ethan's head '…is our son.' Saying the words aloud for the first time sent a quiver of something like pride through Luca's chest.

A smile wreathed Mario's face, transforming him from grizzly bear to teddy bear. 'Nice to meet you, Miss Sinclair,' he said, extending a beefy hand.

Annah hesitated, then put her hand out for a shake. Mario's enormous paw engulfed her slender hand entirely. 'And you,' she said.

Mario looked towards Ethan, who blinked, round-eyed. 'Hello, Ethan.'

Luca said, 'Mario has a daughter about your age, Ethan.'

Ethan's gaze shifted back and forth between the two men. 'What's her name?'

'Liliana,' said Mario.

'That's a pretty name,' Annah remarked, her features relaxing into a smile.

Mario beamed and then, with a nod to Luca, politely took his leave, returning to the SUV.

Annah's eyes met Luca's and her mouth opened, but whatever she intended to say was halted by the approach of a smiling, curly-haired brunette from behind the café's counter. Luca stifled a flare of frustration.

'Hi, Annah,' said the brunette. She sent Luca a polite smile laced with a hint of curiosity. When Annah didn't offer an introduction, the woman ruffled Ethan's hair. 'Hey, young man. Want to see the puppies?'

Ethan grinned. 'Yes!'

'Yes, what?' Annah said gently.

'Yes, please!'

The woman smiled. 'Come out the back, then. Laura's just home from school and having a play now.' She looked at Annah and Luca. 'What can I bring you? Coffee? Something to eat?'

Luca ordered a coffee, and Annah a pot of Earl Grey tea.

Once they were seated and Ethan had disappeared with the woman, Luca said quietly, 'You need to trust me, Annah.'

Her gaze dropped to the blue-and-white-checked tablecloth. 'I'm trying,' she said after a moment. 'It's just…'

'Just what?' he prompted when she didn't finish.

Her eyes came back to his. 'I don't know you, Luca.'

'Then give me the benefit of the doubt,' he said, fighting to keep frustration out of his voice, 'and believe me when I tell you that neither myself nor anyone in my employ will ever harm you or Ethan.'

Her teeth trapped her bottom lip for a moment, drawing his gaze to a mouth he'd tried to forget over the years but hadn't succeeded in banishing from his fantasies.

'What is it?' he said gruffly, shifting slightly in his chair, shocked to find himself aroused by something as simple as Annah biting her lip.

'I heard things,' she said finally, her voice lowering a notch. 'About your father. Things that…scared me.'

'From whom?'

'A friend of a friend—an Italian who has relatives in Sicily.'

'What sort of things?' he said, though he had a fair idea already.

She kept her voice low. 'That he was corrupt. Involved with the wrong kind of people. That he was ruthless, and anyone who got on his bad side needed to watch their backs.' She stared at him, her expression expectant, as though waiting for Luca to brush aside the claims as nothing more than idle gossip.

If only he could.

The café owner arrived with their hot drinks. Luca thanked her and waited until she'd gone before he spoke. 'My father is dead,' he reminded Annah bluntly. 'He is no longer a threat to you or to Ethan. I control Cavallari Enterprises now—and I assure you, things are done very differently under my watch.'

She blinked, but before he could discern either trust or doubt in her eyes, her thick golden-brown lashes swept down and she picked up the teapot and filled her cup. 'So, are you living back in London?'

'No.' He sipped his drink and suppressed a grimace; the English made coffee only marginally better than the Americans. 'Palermo. I moved back in January after my father died.'

She put down the teapot but didn't pick up her cup. 'Are you planning to stay in Sicily, then?'

'For the foreseeable future, yes.'

'Mummy, look!'

At the sound of Ethan's voice, they both turned their heads. He walked over to them, a small golden puppy snuggled in his arms.

Annah smiled and stroked the puppy's head. 'She's adorable.'

'He's a boy,' Ethan corrected. The puppy wriggled and licked Ethan's chin. He giggled. 'I wish we could take him home,' he said, his voice full of longing. 'I think Mister Pickles would like him.'

Annah's smile faltered. Gently but firmly, she said, 'We talked about why we can't have a dog, remember? This little fella will grow big one day, and big dogs need to have a garden and lots of room for running around.'

Ethan sighed heavily. 'I know.' He kissed the puppy's head. 'I better take him back to Sandy.'

When Ethan had gone, Luca raised an eyebrow at Annah. 'Mister Pickles?'

'Cat,' she said.

'Ah.'

Animal, not man.

'Who'd be even less impressed than our landlord if we took home a dog,' she added.

But Luca only half heard that last bit. Why had he not already considered the possibility of a man being on the scene? Annah was a beautiful, desirable woman. Granted, some men balked at taking on another's child. But even so, what was the likelihood of her not having attracted at least one suitor in the last four years?

Nil.

His gut clenched. He had no claim on Annah, yet the idea of her sharing her bed with another man was about as palatable as battery acid.

A brazen demand to know whether or not she had a lover sprang to the tip of his tongue, but then the café door opened and a middle-aged couple entered on a waft of chilly air. The man went to the counter; the woman glanced around and then sat at the window table behind Annah, close enough to overhear their conversation.

Luca bit back the question. 'We need time alone to talk,' he said instead. 'In private, without interruptions. Can you dine with me tomorrow night?'

Annah hesitated. 'I'd need to arrange a babysitter, but...yes.'

'I'm staying at Fendalton Hall. Do you know it?'

Her eyes widened. 'I do.'

'I'll have Mario collect—'

She cut him off. 'No. I'll drive. It's only twenty minutes from Hollyfield, and I'm familiar with the route.'

'All right.' He nodded, satisfied.

Ten minutes later, he waited beside Annah's hatchback while she strapped Ethan into his car seat. Luca had already said goodbye to his son and promised he'd see him again soon—a promise he intended to keep.

Annah straightened and shut the door.

'Give me your phone,' he said.

Her brow puckered.

He added, 'So I can programme my number in.'

She hesitated a few seconds longer but then, with a sigh, pulled her mobile from her jacket, unlocked it, and handed it over.

He thumbed his number in, sent a text to himself, and passed the phone back. 'Now you can reach me any time, day or night.' Then he leaned in and brushed his lips against her temple, allowing his mouth to linger a few pleasurable beats longer than he should have before pulling back. 'I'll see you tomorrow night, yes?'

'Um... Yes.' And then she hurried round to the driver's side, got in without another word or even a glance in his direction, and drove off.

Luca stood and watched until the hatchback was out of sight.

He climbed into the back of the SUV.

'Everything okay, boss?' Mario asked.

Luca relaxed against the seat. 'It will be.'

CHAPTER FOUR

ANNAH CHANGED HER outfit three times before settling on a navy-blue shift dress, a string of pearls with matching earrings, and a pair of taupe pumps.

It was the kind of ensemble she'd wear to a meeting with a wedding client at a posh venue, which made it perfect for this evening because in these parts you didn't get much posher than Fendalton Hall, and her dinner with Luca *was* a meeting, not—as she had reminded herself repeatedly over the last twenty-four hours—a date.

Still, her stomach fluttered with nerves as she spritzed on some perfume, grabbed her handbag and a smart, knee-length black coat to pull on over her dress, and headed to the living room.

Chloe, who had seen the first two outfits and agreed they weren't quite right, jumped up from the sofa, gave the new outfit a once-over, and declared, 'Perfect!'

'Not too much make-up?'

Chloe shook her head. 'Just right. How are you feeling?'

'Fine.'

'You're a terrible liar.'

In spite of herself, Annah laughed. 'And you're an amazing friend. You didn't need to come back early.'

Chloe had called last night to chat and also check some details for a wedding job they were doing on Saturday. Since Chloe knew the history of Ethan's conception and the events that had unfolded afterwards, Annah told her all about Luca showing up and demanding to see their son, not expecting that Chloe would rush back to Hollyfield a day earlier than planned.

'Don't be silly,' Chloe said firmly. 'I want to be here for you.' She dropped back onto the sofa, narrowly missing Mister Pickles, who leapt to the floor with an indignant flick of his ginger tail. 'Anyway, I was dying for some fresh country air after five days in London. And of course Ben's delighted to have me back early.'

Annah felt a jab of guilt. 'Except you're not even spending the evening at home with him. You're here, babysitting for me.'

Chloe waved a hand. 'It's fine. He's still at work. He'll come over and keep me company after his shift ends.' She sent Annah a mock-dramatic look. 'Imagine if I hadn't come back and you'd had to ask Dot to babysit. You know she would have made it her personal mission to find out who you were having dinner with, right?'

'I know,' Annah said, pulling her coat on and

cinching the belt at her waist. 'You're a lifesaver.' She opened her handbag and checked its contents for the nth time. Wallet. Keys. Lip balm. Tissues. Satisfied, she zipped it shut, slid the strap over her shoulder, and glanced down the hallway. 'Is Ethan asleep? Maybe I should check on him before I go.'

'He's dead to the world. Don't risk waking him. You've already checked on him six times. Have you got your phone?'

Her eyes widened. 'Blast!' She dashed back to her bedroom, retrieved her phone from where she'd left it charging, and returned to the living room.

Chloe was on her feet again, rifling through her own bag. 'Hang on a sec,' she said, and then extracted a small object and thrust it towards Annah. 'Take this.'

Annah's eyes zoned in on the object. Her jaw dropped. 'Is that *pepper spray*?'

'No!' Chloe gave her an outraged look. 'Are you kidding? I live with a copper. Ben would kill me—or arrest me—if I had real pepper spray.' She held up the canister. 'This is a perfectly legal defence spray. I never visit London without it.'

Annah frowned and shook her head. 'I don't need that.'

'Are you sure?' Chloe bit her lip. 'I mean, *really* sure? Because this…' she pointed a finger at her face '…this cheerful thing I'm trying to do? It's not working.' Her shoulders slumped and her pretty face creased with genuine concern. 'I'm worried, Annah,' she confessed. 'And so is Ben. How do you know you can trust this guy?'

Annah had asked herself the same question a dozen times. She looked at her friend. 'Honestly? I don't know how I know. I just do. It's a gut feeling, I guess.' And so far, Luca had given her no reason *not* to trust him. He'd behaved like a perfect gentleman yesterday. And the way he'd been with Ethan—so gentle and kind—had brought a lump to her throat. 'I can't explain it,' she said with a one-shouldered shrug. 'But I honestly don't believe he would do anything to harm me or Ethan.'

Chloe vented a heavy sigh. 'Okay, then.' She returned the spray to her bag. 'But if he so much as lays a finger on you—' her expression turned adorably fierce '—he'll have me and Ben and the entire local constabulary to answer to!'

Thirty minutes later, Annah drove up the stately, oak-lined driveway to the entrance of Fendalton Hall. In the darkness she couldn't appreciate the views, but she knew that acres of landscaped grounds and beautiful gardens surrounded her.

An enormous Elizabethan mansion that'd been painstakingly renovated and transformed into an exclusive hotel and spa, Fendalton Hall catered to the kind of guest who could afford to flit in and out for a few days of world-class luxury and indulgent pampering whenever the mood took them.

Several of her and Chloe's past clients—the ones

for whom money was no object—had held their wedding ceremonies and receptions at the beautiful upmarket locale. Impressed with their work, the hotel's manager had contracted Scent Floral Boutique to design and install all the floral arrangements throughout the property.

Annah and Chloe took turns setting up fresh arrangements in the foyer and other areas twice a week, but this was the first time Annah had visited as a patron.

Nervous anticipation hummed through her veins as the big, grey stone manor loomed into view. Carefully, she eased her old-model hatchback into a gap between a low-slung sports car and a luxury sedan. Shutting off the engine, she pulled down her visor and looked in the mirror. Having run out of time to fuss with her hair, she'd pulled it into a low chignon and teased out some wispy bits around her face. She adjusted one of the pins, then grabbed her bag off the passenger seat and headed inside to the restaurant.

After she'd given Luca's name to the maître d', the man took her coat and led her to a candlelit table set with white linen, silver cutlery and sparkling glassware. The restaurant was busy, but the table's location in a secluded corner offered privacy from the other diners.

Luca was already there, and he rose to his feet, tall and shockingly handsome in a white open-necked shirt and dark trousers. He stepped towards her and leaned forward, lightly kissing her cheek, and this time, unlike yesterday, Annah was prepared for the shock of his warm lips against her skin and the resultant flicker of heat that whispered through her.

'You look lovely,' he said.

Pleasure flared at the compliment, though she tried to tamp it down, reminding herself to keep a cool head. Of course Luca was going to lay on the charm. He needed her amenable and co-operative. Ultimately, this was a negotiation; he wanted access to their son, and right now she was the one thing standing between him and Ethan.

'Thank you,' she murmured, and slid into the chair the maître d' had pulled out for her.

The first ten minutes were easy. They ordered drinks, perused the menus, asked their waiter to elaborate on a couple of the dishes, and ordered starters and mains.

And then they were alone.

Immediately, the air thickened.

Annah picked up her glass of Merlot and took a generous sip. She'd have to make a single glass last the entire meal given she was driving, but hopefully a small hit of alcohol on an empty stomach would shave the edge off her nerves.

Luca's deep voice broke the silence. 'Thank you for allowing me to spend time with you and Ethan yesterday. I appreciate this situation isn't easy for you. If it's any consolation, it is not easy for me, either.'

She set her glass down. 'You didn't give me much

choice,' she told him, a frown tugging her eyebrows together. 'Turning up out of the blue like that.'

His gaze sharpened on hers. 'What would you have preferred? A letter from my lawyers?'

Her back snapped straight. *Lawyers?* Was that a warning shot across her bow? Letting her know he hadn't pulled out the big guns but would do so if necessary? 'You would have involved lawyers before you'd even confirmed Ethan was yours?' she challenged.

'If I'd had any doubts that he was mine,' he said, 'then, yes, I'd have had my lawyers formally request a paternity test.'

'So you don't want one anyway?' she couldn't help saying. 'Just to be sure?'

His eyes narrowed. 'Are you telling me Ethan's paternity is in question? Because we can have him tested if necessary.'

Annah swallowed and sat back, her silly challenge falling miserably flat. A paternity test would work in Luca's favour, not against him. 'No,' she said, lifting her wine glass. 'It's not necessary.'

Their waiter turned up a few seconds later with little *amuse bouches* of tuna tartare, saving the moment from growing too tense.

'Who's looking after Ethan tonight?' Luca asked when they were alone again.

'Chloe, my business partner and friend,' she said, trying to match his conversational tone. If he could make an effort to keep things amicable, so could she.

'She's known Ethan since he was born, so she's kind of like an aunty.' Annah thought of the canister of spray Chloe had wanted her to bring. Although she still believed Luca didn't pose any physical threat, she figured it couldn't hurt to add, 'Her boyfriend is a local policeman.'

He sipped his wine, studied her a moment. 'Is Chloe the friend you'd originally planned to start a business with?'

Annah's heart hitched a beat, just like it had yesterday when he'd referenced what she'd once shared with him about wanting to start a business. She canted her head. 'I can't believe you remember what we talked about that night in London.'

He put his glass down, but his eyes stayed on hers. His voice dropped an octave. 'I remember a lot of things about that night, Annah.'

His evocative tone made something low down in her pelvis tighten, and she quickly dropped her gaze, afraid he'd see the truth—that she was still wildly attracted to him—in her eyes.

Sitting across from him now, aware of that little throb in her core, she couldn't believe she'd ever tried to convince herself that he'd shamelessly seduced her that night. That she, in all her virginal innocence, hadn't stood a chance against that lethal mix of searing good looks, blatant sensuality, and irresistible charm.

That was a total cop-out.

She might have been inexperienced, but at twenty-two she'd had plenty of practice saying no to men. Witnessing the train wreck of her mother's love life had made her wary of the opposite sex and she'd routinely rejected any sexual or romantic advances. She'd never really understood how she attracted attention when she didn't give out any signals, but clearly some men found the combination of blonde hair, blue eyes, and a pair of average-sized breasts irresistible.

The truth was, she simply hadn't wanted to say no to Luca. Their chemistry had been intense. Overwhelming. Underneath his charm had been a smouldering intensity that had only enhanced his appeal. Faced with the choice of walking away or taking what he offered, caution and good sense had suddenly seemed overrated.

'Annah?'

She snapped back to the present. 'Sorry?'

'You haven't answered my question,' he said, his dark eyes glittering as if he knew exactly where her thoughts had veered. 'About Chloe.'

She cleared her throat. 'Yes. We trained together and talked about opening a boutique eventually.'

'And neither of you wanted to stay in London?'

She shook her head. 'Too expensive. We'd never have got a business off the ground there. Chloe grew up in these parts and still has family here, so this area was a natural drawcard.' And leaving London had put distance between Annah and Franco Cavallari. Even though she hadn't known if he lived in London full time, just knowing his company had offices there had set her on edge.

Their waiter turned up and placed their starters in front of them. Annah had ordered the crab, and the presentation on the plate was delicate and pretty, the aroma divine. Her appetite stirred. This was an award-winning restaurant and the sort of place she could never afford to dine. It would be a crying shame, she told herself, to not at least try to enjoy the food.

She forked up a morsel, popped it in her mouth, and closed her eyes.

The expression of pleasure on Annah's beautiful face as she enjoyed her food made Luca's blood surge.

He tried to concentrate on his own entrée instead of on her sexy mouth, but it was difficult not to think about the only other time they'd shared a meal— when the food had been delivered by room service, they'd been naked under their bathrobes, and they'd barely made a dent in the fare before earthier appetites lured them back to bed.

In a desperate attempt to divert his thoughts, he asked, 'Is it not difficult to generate business in such a remote area?'

She looked at him and shook her head. 'It's not that remote. Exeter's only a thirty-minute drive away. And this region is popular for weddings. The bulk of our business from spring through to autumn comes from wedding clientele. And we have contracts with a number of venues and hotels in the area—including Fendalton Hall. We usually do at least two weddings here each year,' she added, and then her gaze flicked to where his left hand rested on the table.

A smile tugged at the corners of Luca's mouth. So, she was curious about his marital status? He raised his ringless fingers. 'Not hitched.' He looked at her steadily. Kept his tone casual. 'What about you? Boyfriend?'

Colour rose to her cheeks. 'No. Too busy.' Her gaze shifted away and she shrugged. 'Being a working mother isn't terribly conducive to dating.'

Luca found that news inordinately pleasing—and why shouldn't he? He didn't want another man usurping his role as Ethan's father.

Yet a voice in his head mocked him. It wasn't only about Ethan. It was about Annah. He had taken her virginity and now she was the mother of his child. Some deep-rooted primal instinct that surely harked back to caveman days aroused a desire to stamp his ownership on her and deny any other man the right to touch her.

Annah drew her wine glass in front of her, after the waiter cleared their plates, and toyed with the stem. A frown notched her brow. 'How did you find out that your father had photos of Ethan and me?'

Luca inhaled sharply. 'The photos were discovered after I ordered his apartment in Rome to be cleared out,' he said after a moment.

'You said they're surveillance photos?'

'They appear to be, yes.'

She shook her head, her frown deepening. 'I don't understand. How did he even know about Ethan? He knew I was pregnant obviously, but… How did he know I didn't have an abortion? Unless…'

He watched her expression shift, confusion giving way to dismay and then something resembling horror as she no doubt considered the same possibility he had. That Franco had kept tabs on her from the moment she'd left his office five years ago—meaning she'd been tracked and watched from before Ethan was born to right up until a few months ago.

Reaching over the table, he covered her hand with his. She jumped, but didn't pull her hand away.

Did she feel the same surge of electric warmth from the contact as he did?

'Don't, *cara*,' he said.

She looked down at their joined hands, then back at him. 'Don't what?' she whispered.

'Don't run a million scenarios through your head and wonder which, if any, are true. The answer died with my father—and, like I told you yesterday, so did any threat he might have posed. You and Ethan are safe. You have my word.'

Their mains turned up, and Luca withdrew his hand. For the next few minutes he watched her toy with her food, her mind clearly stuck on their previous conversation.

He put down his knife and picked up his wine. 'Tell me about Ethan.'

She looked up, her head tilting. 'What do you want to know?'

He shrugged. 'Anything. Everything. What's his favourite food?'

A smile curved her mouth. 'I wish I could say peas or broccoli. But unfortunately it's ice cream.'

He chuckled, and she laughed with him, visibly relaxing. And then she talked easily about their son—his preschool programme, his love of animals, his quirks and habits.

When they'd finished their meals and the time was right, he posed a more serious question. 'Did Ethan ever ask about his father?'

She hesitated. 'Yes. A few months ago. He started noticing that most other children had daddies and he didn't.'

'What did you tell him?'

'That sometimes mummies and daddies don't live together. That sometimes children live with only one parent while they grow up.'

'Was he satisfied with that?'

She gave a wry smile. 'Not really. He wanted to know where his father lived and if we could visit. I told him you lived across a big ocean, too far away.'

The waiter returned to remove their plates, and Luca requested a few minutes before they looked at the dessert menu.

Then he leaned forward and finally cut to the chase. 'I want a hand in raising my son, Annah.'

Annah stared at Luca across the table. Over the last hour she'd let herself relax a little, even laugh now and again, but in the back of her mind she'd kept reminding herself this moment was coming.

'Visitation rights?' she ventured.

'Shared custody.'

It wasn't really a surprise, but still her heart dropped into her stomach and then began to pound hard.

'And how would that work, exactly?' she said, willing her voice to stay calm. 'We live in different countries, Luca.'

'Sicily is three hours away by plane.'

'Plus travel time to London, two-hour check-in, travel delays. It's quite a journey for a young boy—and presumably you're suggesting he do this on a regular basis?'

Luca's expression was smooth. Unperturbed. 'He'll travel on my corporate jet via Exeter. As you pointed out yourself, it's only a thirty-minute drive away.'

Of course he'd already worked out the logistics—and of *course* he had a private plane. She sat back. 'He starts school later this year. What then? Do we disrupt his schedule to suit you? Children need structure. Routine.'

'He can come to me in the holidays.' Luca's voice

was calm, but a hard, determined glint shone in his eyes. 'If you're concerned about his schooling, I will arrange for him to have tutors when he's in Sicily.'

Annah's stomach cramped. How foolish she'd been to think she'd come prepared for this conversation. She wasn't prepared in the slightest.

Her mind raced with a hundred questions. A hundred *objections*.

'Will he even be safe in Sicily?'

He frowned. 'Ethan will always be safe with me. I've told you this.'

'Is that why you travel with a bodyguard?'

'Mario is here as my driver.'

'And when you're at home? In Sicily? Is he just a driver then?'

Luca pulled in a breath, blew it out slowly. 'Annah. I know the things you heard about my father frightened you. But he's gone. I am in charge now. Things are different. Better.'

His voice was low and soothing, but she didn't want to be soothed. She wanted all of this to go away. She wanted Luca to disappear as suddenly as he'd arrived. She wanted to keep her beautiful boy all to herself.

A lump formed in her throat. She couldn't lose her little boy. He was everything to her. *Everything.* 'I think I need some air,' she choked out.

He reached a hand across the table, but she pulled her wrist back, her pulse leaping at the very thought of his strong, warm hand touching hers again. She pushed her chair back from the table.

'Where are you going?' he demanded.

'Outside.'

His brow creased. 'It's cold outside.'

'I don't care.' She shot up from the table, turned and almost collided with the waiter delivering their dessert menus. 'Sorry,' she mumbled, and then she fled the restaurant, descended the stairs, and slipped out through a set of French doors that she knew led to a terrace overlooking manicured gardens and a heated pool.

When she finally came to a stop, she breathed deeply, fighting the irritating sting of tears. A sense of futility swept over her. It didn't matter how many arguments or counter-arguments she threw at Luca, he had a ready answer for everything.

And on one thing at least he was right, dammit: it *was* cold out here.

She hunched her shoulders, rubbed her bare arms, and considered her options. She could seek legal advice, but lawyers weren't cheap. And even if the law supported her—which she suspected it might, because surely she wasn't obligated to send her child overseas—Luca could still tie her up with legal proceedings for God knew how long.

And legalities aside, what about the moral dilemma? Was it right to deny Ethan that time with his father?

The back of her neck tingled, and she tensed as

a presence loomed behind her. Then her coat came around her shoulders.

'*Cara.*'

Luca. Still with that crushed-velvet voice that made her melt from the inside out. Annah had a childish urge to plug her fingers in her ears so she couldn't hear him.

Big hands curled around her upper arms and gently pulled her back against a solid, muscular body. 'Don't make this harder than it needs to be,' he said.

She wanted to shrug him off, but he was wonderfully warm, and the too-delicious sensation of being this close to him made her languid and weak-willed. 'It's too much,' she said quietly, staring out over the illuminated gardens. 'Too fast. I need time to get my head around all of this.'

'I don't have time. I need to return to Sicily. I want us to reach an understanding before I go.' He took a deep breath, his chest expanding against her back. 'I've tried to be understanding, Annah. Patient.'

She stiffened. 'Patient? It's been little more than twenty-four hours since you arrived!'

'Which is twenty-four hours more than I can afford to spare,' he said sharply. 'I have obligations, work responsibilities in Sicily.'

'Oh! Well!' She spun, anger uncharacteristically getting the better of her. 'Heaven forbid your son should keep you from your work!' she snapped, pushing her face close to his.

A mistake, she realised two seconds before his

jaw clenched and unclenched and a dangerous cocktail of anger and heat flashed like sheet lightning in his dark eyes. He growled low in his throat, and then he pulled her roughly against him, dipped his head, and covered her mouth with his.

For a second she froze, and then heat slammed through her body, wiping her brain of everything but her awareness of Luca's powerful body flush against hers and the incredible sensation of being kissed by him again after all these years.

It was everything she remembered and more. More intense. More intimate. *Hotter.* So hot she could no longer feel the cold night air against her skin. Before she realised what she was doing, she rose on tiptoe and wrapped her arms around his neck, pressing her breasts against his chest and parting her lips in wanton encouragement.

He went deeper and their tongues tangled intimately—and then the sounds of multiple voices and boisterous laughter carried from the gardens below.

Their mouths jerked apart.

Shocked back to her senses, Annah pulled out of his embrace.

Luca swore in Italian and shoved his hand through his hair.

On trembling legs, Annah turned back to the view of the pool and gardens, leaning against the wrought-iron railing for support, her whole body quivering in the aftermath of their kiss.

After a long moment, Luca came and stood beside her, his hands gripping the iron railing. 'Is this what you want for Ethan?' he said in a low, controlled voice. 'Two parents arguing over him?'

'No,' she whispered, feeling drained and utterly wretched all of a sudden. 'It's not.'

Silence reigned for a full minute.

'Come to Sicily,' Luca said.

She turned her head to look at him. 'What?'

'Bring Ethan for a holiday. Stay for a week, two weeks, however long you want. You can see the family estate for yourself. See that it's safe. We'll have more time to discuss custody arrangements. And you can meet my mother.'

His mother. *The wife of Franco Cavallari.*

As if he'd read her thoughts, Luca said, 'She didn't know about you or Ethan. She was devastated to learn what my father had done. It would mean a lot to her to meet her grandson.'

Annah pursed her lips. Emotional blackmail? *Unfair.* 'When?'

'Return with me tomorrow.'

She stared at him. 'I can't. Chloe and I are doing a wedding on Saturday. And Ethan and I don't even have passports.'

'I can expedite those. How long will you need on Saturday?'

'We're usually done by midday.'

'Then we can fly in the afternoon.'

Annah's head spun at a dizzying rate. Private jets. Expedited passports. A week in Sicily.

A little voice told her she could say no, but what then?

Luca was in her and Ethan's lives now, and he'd made it abundantly clear he wasn't going away. Sooner or later she'd have to deal with him—or his lawyers.

She dragged in a breath of the cool night air and puffed it out on a single word of surrender. 'Okay.'

CHAPTER FIVE

By THREE-FIFTEEN P.M. on Saturday, Luca's jet was cruising above the clouds over continental Europe, one hour and fifteen minutes into its three-hour flight from Exeter to Palermo.

He looked up from his laptop, his focus shifting from the report on his screen to Annah as she emerged from the bedroom at the rear of the aircraft and returned to the lounge area in sock-clad feet.

She wore a pale grey soft jersey top and stretchy black leggings that moulded to her long legs like a second skin. She'd probably chosen the outfit for comfort over style or sex appeal, but Luca's body hummed with appreciation nevertheless, ratcheting up the desire that had burned like a low-grade fever in his blood ever since his self-control had slipped and he'd kissed her on the terrace at Fendalton Hall.

'Is he asleep?' he asked.

'Yes.' She dropped into the leather recliner opposite him where she'd spent the first hour of the flight either reading a magazine or entertaining Ethan in the seat next to hers. She produced a tired-looking smile. 'He doesn't usually need an afternoon nap, but last night he was so excited about the trip I couldn't get him to sleep.'

He scrutinised her face. Judging from the blue shadows underscoring her eyes, she hadn't got much sleep, either.

Guilt flickered for a moment before he ruthlessly shut it down. He knew he was pushing hard, urging things forward at a pace she was struggling to accept. He wasn't unsympathetic to her position, but she needed to appreciate *his* position. He had missed the first four years of his son's life. He wasn't prepared to sit back and wait weeks or months for her to get comfortable with the idea of his claiming his parental rights.

Luca knew the brutal cost of not being there for the people he had a responsibility to protect.

Never again.

He closed his laptop and set it aside. Suggesting she bring Ethan to Sicily was, he'd thought, a fair and generous solution. It gave them additional face-time to discuss and agree on a shared custody arrangement, while she essentially got an all-expenses-paid, week-long vacation and he got to see more of Ethan.

Win-win.

Except they weren't going to get anywhere fast if Annah kept her barriers up and didn't start to trust him.

'And you?' he enquired. 'How did you sleep?'

She lifted a slim shoulder. 'I've never been a good sleeper.'

'Even as a child?' he said, realising he knew nothing at all about her childhood or family background.

She tucked her feet under her. Long suede boots had accompanied her outfit, but she'd removed them shortly after take-off. 'Yes. But Ethan's a good sleeper ordinarily. Once he's out, nothing wakes him.' A hint of curiosity entered her blue eyes. 'I sometimes wondered if he might have inherited that from you.'

Luca cast his mind back to his early childhood. At thirty he was hardly an old-timer, but those days of boyhood innocence felt like several lifetimes ago.

'I was an extremely sound sleeper,' he said, the recollection surprising him. He found his lips curving into a smile. 'My mother used to say she could put me on Mount Etna during an eruption and I still wouldn't wake.' As quickly as it emerged, his smile faded. That had been a different time for him and his mother. A happier time. Now they were the only ones left, and some days they barely exchanged a word. 'It's different now,' he said. 'I only ever sleep for a few hours at a time. When I lived in New York, I rarely got more than four to five hours a night.'

Her head tilted to the side. 'What did you do there?'

'Dabbled in stocks, backed a couple of technology start-ups that went big, then started my own private equity firm.'

Her eyebrows lifted. 'So you're running two companies now?'

'No.' Although he had tried and then realised within weeks it wasn't feasible. Legitimising the family business, weeding out the corruption, was a gruelling full-time endeavour. 'I've recently appointed a CEO to replace me in New York.'

'Did you ever visit Sicily?' she asked. 'In those five years you lived in America?'

He hesitated. 'Once.'

'And you didn't speak to your father then?'

'No.'

'Why did you go back?'

Discomfort pressed on his chest. He'd wanted to get Annah talking about herself. Instead, she'd turned the tables somehow and they were talking about him. 'For my brother's funeral,' he told her.

Shock spread over her features, followed swiftly by sympathy. 'I'm so sorry, Luca.'

'It was three years ago,' he said, his tone dismissive, as if his brother's violent, totally unavoidable death was ancient history and not still a dark, festering wound on his soul.

The plane juddered briefly, rattling a glass of water on the table beside him before stabilising again.

Annah's hands gripped her armrests so tightly, the skin over her knuckles appeared in danger of splitting.

'It's only turbulence,' he reassured her.

She nodded, her grip on the chair easing. 'I'm not used to flying.'

He frowned. He'd put her lack of a passport down to her having let an old one expire, as opposed to being a novice traveller. 'You've never flown before?'

'Only once. A long time ago.'

Her wan smile stirred an acute craving in him to see the more radiant version he knew existed. The one so incandescent it could chase the shadows from the corners of the darkest room—or the blackest soul.

He waited for her to elaborate.

She didn't.

'A family holiday?' he prompted, her reticence becoming a touch irksome. Women *liked* to talk, didn't they?

'A school trip.' She unfolded her legs, as long as a model's but without that stick-insect look he'd never found appealing. Annah's legs actually had definition and shape. 'I should check on Ethan.'

'It's only been a few minutes,' he pointed out.

'I know.' Her gaze skipped away from his. 'But the turbulence might have woken him. It's *his* first time on a plane.'

Luca stood. 'Relax. I'll go.'

'No.' She jumped up. 'It's all right. I— Oh!'

The plane jolted as they hit another rough pocket of air. Like before, the turbulence lasted only seconds, but the motion was more jarring this time, ending with a sharp dip and bump.

Luca kept his footing, but Annah stumbled and pitched forward—straight into his arms. Her hands landed on his chest; his went to her hips to steady her, settling over luscious curves that enticed him to pull her closer, not set her away.

He didn't move, and neither did Annah. She stared up at him, her face scant inches from his.

His brain said *let go*.

His body said *don't*.

His hands—as if they weren't attached to a man who prided himself on his self-control and his ability to resist his baser urges—strengthened their hold, his thumbs finding the delicate protrusion of her hip bones and his fingers splaying until his pinkies brushed the swell of her backside.

Her pupils dilated, her gaze dropped to his mouth, and an unmistakable flush of desire stained her cheeks.

A corresponding heat blasted through Luca's body. A visceral acknowledgement of the stunning chemistry between them. He wanted to kiss her again like he had the other night and to hell with the complications.

'Signor Cavallari?'

A soft female voice, respectful and slightly apologetic, came from behind him. He felt Annah's body tense and then she blinked, snatched her hands off his chest and stepped back as if he were suddenly radioactive.

Cursing inwardly, willing the heat inside him to

disperse, he turned to look at his flight attendant. 'Yes?'

'The pilot is anticipating more turbulence,' she informed him. 'He suggests everyone fasten their seat belts for the next half-hour.'

He nodded. 'Thank you.'

Annah said, 'I'll get Ethan.'

'I will,' he told her. 'Sit down and strap in.'

Her forehead creased. 'Don't give me orders, Luca. Not where it concerns Ethan. I'm his mother.'

'And I am his father,' he said, a surge of frustration sharpening his tone. Was this how it would always be? Her getting her hackles up over every tiny thing? Getting possessive over their son? 'Ethan is as much my responsibility as he is yours. The sooner you come to terms with that, the easier this will be for all of us—including Ethan.'

Luca brushed past her and strode to the bedroom. His heart pounded. His blood thrummed in his veins. How did she manage to anger him and kindle his desire to kiss her at the same time? He had no answer. No logical one, at any rate.

And that irritated him even more.

The sight of Luca holding a sleepy Ethan in his strong arms made something shift in Annah's chest.

Given that he was a bachelor who probably had little to no experience with children, she hadn't expected him to look as comfortable as he did carrying Ethan, neither had she expected Ethan to look quite so content in Luca's arms.

As they got closer, Ethan blinked sleepy eyes at her, and she waited for him to hold out his arms to her, but they remained looped around Luca's neck.

She looked at them both. Two dark heads. Two sets of beautiful, dark brown eyes—one pair completely innocent and trusting, the other wiser and disconcertingly astute.

Somehow, man and boy looked right together.

Like father and son.

Inwardly, Annah sighed. It was beyond silly to feel jealous and possessive. She was Ethan's mother and nothing was going to change that. But up until three days ago she'd been the only parent her son had ever known, and now, suddenly, Luca was encroaching on her territory. It made her want to draw a firm boundary around her and Ethan and shove Luca onto the other side of it.

Together, she and Luca settled Ethan into the seat beside hers, reclining it before tucking a blanket around him and then fastening the seat belt over the top. She kissed his forehead and stroked her fingertips through his hair. Within minutes he was asleep again, despite the juddering of the plane each time they hit another turbulent pocket of air.

Settling back in her own seat, she picked up a magazine and leafed through it. The words were a blur and even the pictures were difficult to focus on, but it was better than resuming her conversation with

Luca, which had got too close to things she didn't like talking about.

Would he think her capable of being a good mother if he knew she'd barely spoken with her own in the last few years? Not that he was in any position to judge. By his own account, he hadn't spoken with his father in the five years before Franco Cavallari had died. But for all her sins, Rachel Sinclair could hardly be compared to the likes of Luca's father. She wasn't inherently bad. She was simply self-absorbed, incapable of seeing beyond the scope of her own needs and desires, too emotionally needy and lacking in courage to believe she could ever stand on her own two feet without a man propping her up. Invariably, it was her insecurities that drove men away.

Annah doubted her mother would ever possess enough self-awareness to alter her behaviour, but at least Annah had learned from her mother's mistakes. *She* would never be weak and needy, incapable of looking after herself and her child.

As for divulging the fact that her father was some random guy her mother had slept with after a drunken party when she was eighteen... *No.* She couldn't bear to share that mortifying bit of information. Not when it was the one mistake of her mother's she hadn't avoided making herself. And to think she had once felt superior on that front. Had sat on her lofty moral high ground and looked down upon her mother's behaviour with disgust and scorn. Rachel Sinclair hadn't even made it out of her teens without getting pregnant, while Annah had reached the age of twenty-two with her virginity and her self-respect intact.

And then she'd met Luca and taken a spectacular and rather humbling tumble off her self-appointed pedestal.

To give credit where it was due, Rachel hadn't said anything snide when she'd learnt of Annah's pregnancy, but then she hadn't said anything much at all aside from stressing that she wasn't in a position to provide any support—which was laughable considering Annah hadn't lived with her mother since she'd turned eighteen and had pretty much looked after herself since well before then.

No. Her mother hadn't been there for her at all. It was Chloe and her family who'd helped her during her pregnancy and afterwards, on those rare occasions when necessity and the welfare of her child had demanded she swallow her pride and accept assistance.

She put the magazine down, having reached the end and absorbed not a single word, then picked up another from the pile the flight attendant had left.

She didn't know where she'd be without Chloe, although she'd half hoped her friend would talk her out of taking Ethan to Sicily. After Annah had recounted the essential parts of her and Luca's conversation, however, Chloe had chewed on her thumbnail and conceded that perhaps it wasn't such a bad way forward if Annah wanted to avoid getting the authorities and a bunch of lawyers involved. She'd also assured Annah the boutique would survive without her for a week.

Turning the page of her magazine, Annah sneaked a look at Luca from under her lashes. He'd gone back to his laptop and his eyebrows were scrunched in concentration. Dressed in dark jeans and a pale blue shirt with the collar unbuttoned and the sleeves rolled up his forearms, he looked mouth-wateringly gorgeous.

She skimmed her gaze down his length, all the way to his Italian loafers and back up to the dark film of stubble coating his jaw.

Every part of him looked strong and toned and masculine. His thighs. His arms. His chest.

His chest.

She gripped the magazine and stared blindly at some travel article, her palms tingling as she recalled how that broad expanse of muscle had felt beneath her hands. She hadn't stumbled against him on purpose, but once she was there she hadn't wanted to step away.

And neither had he.

She'd felt it in the increased pressure of his hands on her hips. Seen it in the dark glitter of his eyes. Even through her clothing his fingers had left a burning imprint.

She'd wanted him to kiss her again like he had two nights ago at Fendalton Hall.

Heat pulsed between her thighs and she squirmed

in her seat. She tried to think about something else and her mind landed on Luca's revelation about his brother. Her heart surged again with sympathy.

She'd wondered how he'd died, but Luca's expression had quickly grown shuttered and she hadn't wanted to pry. And she couldn't expect him to open up about his family when she wasn't willing to do so herself.

Which left only one subject on which they could safely converse—their son—and those discussions weren't going to be easy.

Stifling a sigh, she stopped sneaking looks at Luca and buried her nose deeper in the magazine.

It was going to be a very challenging week.

They landed in Palermo just before five p.m., by which time Ethan was wide awake and full of his usual vigour. Annah knelt on the floor to slip his shoes back on, glad to be on solid ground again.

'Are we there?' he asked.

Luca fielded the question from behind her. 'Nearly. We're going to ride in a car now for twenty minutes.'

Ethan huffed out a big sigh. 'It's a long way from our house to your house, isn't it?'

'Yes, but this next part is more interesting. We'll drive past fishing villages and beaches. You'll see more from the car than you did from the plane.'

Ethan's eyes lit up. He looked at Annah. 'Can we go to the beach, Mummy?'

She tugged a sweatshirt over his head. 'Not today, sweetheart,' she said, helping him work his arms into the sleeves. 'It's too late in the afternoon.'

His expression fell. He swung his gaze back to Luca as if hoping his father might offer a more favourable answer.

'Your mother is right,' Luca said. 'But we can go tomorrow—if your mum agrees.'

Ethan brightened. He looked to Annah. 'Can we, Mummy?'

'Yes,' she said, his irrepressible enthusiasm drawing a smile from her. 'I don't see why not.' She pushed to her feet and, grateful that Luca hadn't contradicted her in front of their son, sent him a quick smile. 'Thanks.'

'Of course,' he said, his gaze lingering on hers until she looked away and busied herself with gathering up her and Ethan's things.

After they disembarked, an immigration official checked their passports and then they crossed the tarmac and climbed into a big SUV with shiny black paintwork, tinted windows, and a plush leather interior complete with a child's seat installed for Ethan. Mario, who must have sat in a different part of the plane because she'd scarcely seen him during the flight, rode up front beside the driver, while she, Luca, and Ethan travelled in the back, separated from the men by a dark glass privacy screen.

How the other half lives, she mused, the enormity

of the chasm between her world and Luca's starting to sink in.

A ripple of uneasiness moved through her. Ethan was too young right now to appreciate the perks of his father's wealth, but what would happen as he grew older? At the tender age of four he loved puppies and ice cream and walks in the woods with his mummy. But in ten years things would be different. Her little boy would be a teenager, his interests more likely to run to fast cars, expensive tech, and pretty girls.

Would Luca buy his way into their son's heart?

Jealousy fired a hot streak through her chest. What if Ethan decided one day that he'd rather live with his father? What then? If she let him go, she'd lose him. If she tried to stop him, he'd resent her.

'Look at the boats, Mummy!'

Sucking air into lungs gone painfully tight, she sidelined her thoughts and forced her attention on the scenery. They were passing through one of the fishing villages Luca had mentioned. To their left, pretty pastel-coloured houses huddled against the base of a limestone cliff. On the right, moored to an old stone jetty, a dozen or so small boats rocked gently on the sea, their wooden hulls painted in colourful combinations of blue, white, orange, and green.

Luca was right. The scenery was picturesque—and too lovely to ignore.

After another few minutes they left the coastal road and travelled inland through sun-dappled pine woods and then acres of open countryside. A couple of miles in, the driver turned off the road and stopped before a heavy wrought-iron security gate flanked by a six-foot-high stone wall that ran in both directions as far as she could see.

On the wall, black cast-iron letters spelt out 'Tenuta Cavallari.' *Cavallari Estate.*

The driver reached his arm out and punched a code into a keypad affixed to a freestanding stone column.

And then they were moving again, the vehicle picking up speed as they travelled along a sealed road through a lush landscape of meadows, orchards, and olive groves.

Annah tried not to let her eyes pop.

Or her mouth gape.

She eyed the long, perfectly straight rows of grapevines on the hills out to the east. 'Do you make wine to sell commercially?' she asked, swivelling her gaze to meet Luca's over the top of Ethan's head.

'Yes. We export mainly within the EU, plus a small amount to North America. Our chief wine-maker has worked for the family for over thirty years.' He indicated the extensive olive groves on the other side of the valley. 'We export our olive oils, too.'

Although Annah preferred not to think about her visit to the Cavallari Enterprises offices in London, she cast her mind back and tried to recall what the company specialised in. 'Isn't the company's main business transportation?'

'Yes. And warehousing.'

'So the olive oil and winemaking are just side businesses?'

'They have been up until now. But I intend to expand both operations so they're competitive with the largest producers on the island.'

She wondered if that was Luca's way of stamping his mark on the family business. A deliberate move to take things in a different direction than his father had. She looked out across the valley. 'Where's the winery?'

'On another part of the estate. It has its own access so people can buy direct from the cellar door at certain times of the year.'

She turned back to Luca. 'I can imagine people falling over themselves to hold their wedding receptions or private functions in a setting like this,' she said, enthusiasm creeping into her voice despite herself. 'If you offered a venue as stunning as the surroundings, I'm sure you'd have a flood of interest.'

Luca raised his eyebrows. 'My winery manager said something remarkably similar when he presented his expansion plan recently.'

Annah turned her gaze out the window again, picturing a romantic wedding with the vines and the green hills and olive groves as a backdrop.

Ironically, given she often worked with brides, she didn't think of herself as romantic. Who had time for romance with a business to run and a child to raise single-handedly? That wasn't to say she didn't feel happy for her clients. She did. But a small, cynical part of her always wondered how long each marriage would last. If the couple's love would be strong enough to weather the inevitable storms of life. Her mother seemed to fall in and out of love at the drop of a hat, although Annah suspected it wasn't so much the man but the illusion of security and the thrill of being wanted that Rachel Sinclair fell in love with.

Annah's cynical outlook on relationships horrified Chloe, but Chloe was lucky. She had amazing parents who still adored each other after thirty years of marriage. An older brother blissfully married to his high school sweetheart, their third child on the way.

It was easy to believe in happily-ever-after when you grew up surrounded by it.

Not so easy when your mother was an incurable relationship junkie.

The SUV crested another rise and a stone wall similar to the one at the estate's perimeter came into view. Annah craned her neck and saw another wrought-iron gate ahead, this one more decorative than the last. It slid open as they approached, and she glimpsed a man on the other side. She peered at him through the window, tension creeping down her spine. Was he wearing a shoulder holster with a *gun*?

The SUV stopped and the man braced his hands on its roof and ducked his head to speak with Mario. Annah's chest tightened. She hadn't imagined it;

tucked against the man's side under his left arm, secured in a leather holster, was a handgun.

A chill swept through her body.

The estate is perfectly safe. Wasn't that what Luca had told her? Or, if not those exact words, something to that effect?

If it was safe, why was it guarded by armed men?

A gut-churning mix of anxiety and anger turned her body hot and then cold again. She clenched her hands and jammed them under her arms to hide their trembling. She dared not look at Luca in case fury showed on her face and Ethan witnessed it.

The SUV moved again, climbing a long driveway lined with tall cypress trees before stopping in a gravelled courtyard in front of a huge villa.

Annah threw off her seat belt and unbuckled Ethan. She sensed Luca trying to catch her eye but ignored him. Mario opened her door. She climbed out and turned to reach for Ethan, but he was already scrambling out unaided. And then Luca was beside her, his hand brushing the small of her back to guide her forward. Anger and a sizzling awareness of his touch had her spine stiffening. Avoiding his probing gaze, she took hold of Ethan's hand, anchoring herself with the familiar feel of her son's little fingers tucked within hers.

At the villa's entrance stood an older man in a smart suit and two women in domestic uniforms.

'Annah, this is Victor,' Luca said smoothly. 'Our butler and the head of the household staff.'

Victor gave her a pleasant smile and she wondered if he was packing a gun beneath his pinstriped suit. He extended his hand. 'Welcome, Miss Sinclair.'

Stretching her mouth into something she hoped resembled a smile, Annah shook his hand and managed a polite, 'Thank you.'

Victor's attention turned to Ethan and for a moment the man's expression was utterly arrested. He quietly cleared his throat and leaned down. 'And this must be Master Ethan.'

Ethan slipped his hand from Annah's and stuck it out. 'It's just Ethan,' he told the butler, drawing looks of amusement from the adults around him. Even the stern expression worn by the older of the two women softened.

'Just Ethan it is.' Victor's eyes twinkled, but his tone indulged rather than mocked, and it occurred to Annah that everyone here knew who Ethan was. That he was their employer's son—a Cavallari regardless of what surname he bore—and, as such, would be afforded a certain level of respect.

Victor straightened, then introduced the women. The elder of the two was the housekeeper, Gabriela, who confined her greeting to a courteous dip of her head. The younger woman, Celeste, had a nervous smile but, like Victor, a good grasp of English.

Victor said, 'Celeste will be your personal maid while you're here.'

Annah couldn't imagine why she'd need a personal maid but, not wanting to offend the girl, she kept the thought to herself.

'Where is my mother?' asked Luca.

'She is unwell,' Victor said. 'A headache.' He sent Annah a look of apology. 'Signora Cavallari asked me to express her regret that she is unable to greet you. She looks forward to meeting you when she is feeling better.' He looked at Luca. 'I am afraid she will not be dining with you this evening.'

Luca's expression tightened. 'Very well.' He turned to Annah. 'Celeste will get you and Ethan settled into your rooms. What time does Ethan have his evening meal?'

'Soon.'

He checked his watch. 'I need to do a couple of hours' work.' His gaze lifted to hers. 'Will you join me for supper once Ethan's asleep?'

A churlish part of her wanted to say no. To cry off with a headache like his mother had. Or tell him she simply wasn't in the mood for his company. But she was conscious of his staff listening to their exchange. She nodded. 'Fine.'

His features relaxed a fraction. 'Good. In the meantime, let Celeste know if you need anything. If you'd like something specific prepared for Ethan's meal, tell Celeste and she'll instruct—' His gaze darted to a point beyond her shoulder. 'Ethan!'

Luca's shout made Annah jump. Heart catapulting into her throat, she swung around. Ethan was frozen in the act of walking towards a large Doberman, his arm raised as if to pat the dog's head. That the Doberman was on a leash and restrained by a guard, who was already moving to place himself between Ethan and the animal, didn't lessen Annah's alarm.

She rushed over and scooped Ethan up. His bottom lip quivered. 'It's all right, sweetheart.' She propped him on her hip, hoping he couldn't feel her heart pounding furiously against her chest. 'You're not in trouble. We just don't want you to touch the dog. It's a working dog, not a pet.' She threw Luca a dark look, strode past him, and spoke to Celeste. 'Would you please show us to our rooms now?'

The girl's eyes flicked nervously to Luca and then back to Annah. '*Sì*. Of course.'

She felt the weight of Luca's gaze pressing on her back like a hot hand as she followed Celeste into the villa. She gritted her teeth against the tingling that raced up her spine. How could her body react when he wasn't even touching her? She was too aware of him. Too distracted by the sensations he stirred within her. Why else had she lowered her guard enough to let him talk her into bringing Ethan here?

A mistake.

One she planned to rectify at the first opportunity.

CHAPTER SIX

Luca lifted his wine glass from the table, took a long sip, and watched Annah shuffle a piece of stuffed artichoke from one side of her plate to the other with her fork.

She had turned up for dinner wearing no jewellery, no make-up, a trousers-and-top outfit all in black, and a ponytail that pulled her blonde hair back in a rather severe fashion.

Luca wondered if her stark appearance was a deliberate choice to reflect her mood.

Whatever her intent, the end result didn't diminish her beauty.

It occurred to him that if his mother had bothered to make an appearance, she and Annah would have co-ordinated perfectly given that Eva Cavallari had worn nothing but black since her husband's death.

The perfect mourning widow, Luca thought grimly. As meekly dutiful now as when her husband had been alive.

He pushed aside thoughts of his mother.

'If you're not going to eat,' he said in a mild tone,

'you might as well talk instead and tell me what's wrong.'

She looked up, her blue eyes bright and hard as they connected with his. A dusky pink flared along her cheekbones and her lips grew slightly pursed.

Appreciation surged. Even when angry, she was lovely. His gaze dropped to her mouth and lingered, his mind conjuring other uses for those lush, delectable lips besides eating and talking.

'I want to take Ethan home,' she said abruptly, halting the carnal direction of his thoughts. 'Tomorrow.'

He lifted his eyes back to hers. Put his wine glass down. He wasn't entirely surprised. The deterioration in her mood as soon as they'd arrived at the villa had warned him something was wrong. 'That's not going to happen,' he told her, keeping his voice level.

She dropped her fork on the plate with a clatter. 'Are Ethan and I prisoners here, Luca? Was that your plan all along? To kidnap your son?'

Luca sat back, braced his palms on the table, and spoke softly. 'I'm going to pretend I didn't hear that.'

'Why?' She crossed her arms over her chest. 'So you can avoid answering the question?'

He ground his teeth, summoning patience. 'You and Ethan are not prisoners here. You are free to leave whenever you wish.' He paused. 'Is that what you want, Annah? To take my son away before I've had a chance to know him?'

She shook her head. 'Oh, no. You don't get to lay a guilt trip on me.'

Luca exhaled through his nose. 'I'm not trying to. I want the same thing you do—what's best for our son.'

Annah mirrored his pose, putting her hands on the table. But hers were clenched into white-knuckled fists. 'I'm Ethan's mother. It's my job to know what's best for him. To protect him.'

'And you don't think I take that same responsibility seriously?'

Her eyes held his and then dropped as if she didn't want to acknowledge that he might actually have it in him to be a decent father.

The silence stretched. Frustration gnawed at him. 'For God's sake, Annah. Talk to me. We need to find some middle ground here. We can't achieve that if you won't communicate.'

Her eyes came back to his. Accusation flashed in their sapphire depths. 'You told me it was safe here.'

Ah. Now they were getting somewhere.

'You and Ethan are as safe here as you would be anywhere else,' he assured her.

The look she threw him was a blistering mix of scorn and scepticism. 'Safe because your home is protected by ten-foot walls, men with guns and vicious dogs—one of which could have taken Ethan's hand off this afternoon?'

'That was never going to happen.'

'Is that why you shouted at him?' Her voice filled with reproach. 'You frightened him, Luca.'

Regret burrowed into his conscience. In hindsight, his reaction had been over the top and unnecessary. The dogs were well trained and only attacked on command. His guards would never allow a child to be hurt. He knew all this, yet in that split second when his son's hand had reached towards the Doberman's lethal jaws, he'd reacted not rationally but with the knee-jerk protectiveness of a parent. 'I overreacted,' he confessed. 'Ethan was never in any danger.'

She shook her head, unconvinced. 'I'm sorry, but this isn't the kind of world I want Ethan exposed to.'

He set his jaw. 'That's not entirely your decision to make.'

'Excuse me?'

'I'm his father—'

'Who hasn't been around for the first four years of his son's life.'

'Which is not my fault!' he exploded.

Annah flinched and pulled her hands off the table. 'It's not mine, either,' she whispered.

Luca ran his palm over his face and silently cursed his momentary loss of control. 'I'm sorry. I should not have shouted.'

She pushed back her chair and stood. 'I'm sorry, too. I've lost my appetite.'

She walked around the end of the formal dining table towards the door. Luca rose quickly and blocked her path. When she went to step around him, he put his hands on her upper arms to restrain her.

'Our son is half-Sicilian,' he said quietly, tilting his head to catch her eye. 'Half-Cavallari. He belongs here, in my world, as much as he belongs with you in England.'

She twisted her face to the side, her eyes skating away from his. Because she knew he spoke the truth?

He trailed his gaze down the slender length of her neck.

The sudden thought of setting his mouth against her creamy flesh, sliding his tongue over the sensitive spot between neck and shoulder that he knew would make her body bow with pleasure, was so powerful his hands tightened reflexively on her biceps and drew her closer.

Her gaze snapped back to his and awareness arced in the air like a zap of electricity.

He wanted her. As desperately and urgently as he'd wanted her five years ago in London.

But he couldn't afford to act on his urges. He needed her trust. Her co-operation. With or without it, he would claim his parental rights, but he'd rather not have to do so via an acrimonious custody battle.

Exerting as much self-control as he could muster, he settled for pressing a kiss to her temple.

He closed his eyes for a second. Her skin felt soft and warm against his lips and her subtle floral scent enveloped his senses. His nerve endings leapt. It was all he could do to set her away from him. He looked down at her. 'Stay. Give me the week you promised. I'll show you that your concerns are unfounded.'

He watched the delicate cords in her throat work.

Finally, she blew out a breath and nodded. 'All right.' She glanced at their unfinished meals. 'I'm sorry about dinner, but it was an early start this morning with the wedding and I'm tired. And it's Ethan's first night in unfamiliar surroundings. If he wakes and finds me gone…'

Luca shoved his hands in his trouser pockets as she rattled off her excuses to escape his company. He shrugged. 'Go. Rest. I'll see you tomorrow.'

Relief washed across her features. Without another word, she turned and fled the room. Luca watched her go, then glanced at the table. He too had lost his appetite for food. Too bad his other hunger hadn't waned. Unfortunately, he knew only two solutions for that—satisfy it or kill it. Resigning himself to the latter, he headed to his room for a cold shower.

Coward.

The word echoed in Annah's head as she hurried away from the formal dining room and ascended the sweeping staircase to the second floor, where her and Ethan's suite of rooms was located.

She'd nursed her anger for a good two hours before dinner and then, when she'd finally had the opportunity to express it, to verbalise her feelings, her attempt had been feeble. *Pathetic.*

The trouble was, she had no experience dealing with conflict. She was an only child. Her mother hadn't been around half the time when she was growing up. She had no siblings to argue with. When problems had arisen she'd faced them alone, internalising her emotions because she'd had no one to confide in.

At a young age, she had learned to be self-sufficient.

Since then, her business partnership with Chloe had taught her about teamwork, but she and Chloe shared a similar work ethic and rarely disagreed on anything. When they did, neither got angry and a civilised conversation over a glass of wine usually did the trick.

With a deep sigh, she pushed open the door to the bedroom that was so lovely she'd gasped the first time she'd walked into it. Pale sea-green walls, handcrafted furniture and a big bed covered in gorgeous, snowy linens had filled her with reluctant delight—as had the adjoining sitting room with its balcony overlooking the landscaped gardens, and the connected bedroom for Ethan that was slightly smaller but no less sumptuous.

She pulled up short at the sight of her suitcase open on the floor. Celeste turned around, a bundle of Annah's underwear clutched in her hand.

'What are you doing?' Annah said.

'Unpacking your things.' The maid's smile was tinged with disappointment. 'I thought you would be gone longer. I wanted to have it done before you got back.'

Annah strode over and quickly relieved Celeste of the underwear items, most of which were old, faded pairs of plain cotton knickers. Her cheeks turned hot with embarrassment. 'Thank you. But that's not necessary.' She was perfectly capable of unpacking her own bag and would have done so already had she not convinced herself that she and Ethan were going home tomorrow.

She frowned at the thought of how easily Luca had changed her mind.

One shiver-inducing brush of his lips against her temple and she'd turned into a weak-kneed pushover.

Blast him for being so hard to hate! Why couldn't he be a horrible, despicable man like his father? Why did he have to make everything he asked of her sound so reasonable? Why couldn't he be ugly and repulsive instead of mouth-wateringly gorgeous and drenched in sex appeal?

She stuffed her very unsexy knickers into a drawer, dismissed Celeste as nicely as she could, then kicked off her shoes and padded into Ethan's room to check on him.

He was fast asleep, exactly as she'd left him, his tiny figure dwarfed by the enormous bed. The indentation in the quilt, where she'd fallen asleep beside him, was still visible. If she hadn't dozed off, she would have had more time to prepare herself for dinner. As it was she'd had less than five minutes to make herself presentable.

Not that how she looked mattered. She had no need or desire to doll herself up for Luca.

Leaving the door between the bedrooms open,

she slipped into her comfy PJs, brushed her teeth, crawled beneath the soft cotton sheets in the pretty sea-green room and stared up at the ceiling. She yawned, exhausted yet wired at the same time. It would probably take her hours to go to sleep, she thought glumly.

Within minutes, slumber claimed her.

Annah awoke to the sound of curtains and shutters being opened. A flood of bright sunlight pierced her eyelids, and she bolted upright and blinked.

'Good morning!'

Celeste's cheerful voice made her wince. She focused her eyes on the perky maid as she tucked a turquoise drape behind a gold filigree holdback.

'What time is it?' Annah asked.

'Eight o'clock.' Celeste turned, a look of concern crossing her face. 'This is when you wanted your breakfast, *si*?'

Annah shook off the groggy vestiges of sleep. 'Yes,' she said, vaguely recalling Celeste asking her the question yesterday. But she had planned to be up and dressed by now. Ethan was normally awake by seven. Her gaze flew to the connecting door between the bedrooms.

'He is playing in the sitting room,' Celeste said, guessing the direction of Annah's thoughts.

Annah threw back the bedcovers. 'I should get him washed and dressed.'

'He has already done it,' Celeste informed her,

smiling broadly. 'Mostly on his own, but I gave him
a little help.'

'Oh.' Annah wasn't sure how she felt about that.
She was the only one who'd ever helped her son with
his morning routine.

'Your breakfast is in the sitting room,' Celeste
said. 'I will come back in half an hour to see if there
is anything else you need.' She turned to go, then
stopped and swung back, eyes wide. 'Oh, and there
is a note for you from Signor Cavallari! I left it with
the breakfast things.'

The second Celeste was gone, Annah jumped out
of bed, dragged a sweatshirt on over her PJs, and hurried through to the sitting room.

'Mummy!'

Ethan dropped the magnetic drawing board he
was playing with and launched himself at her.

'Hey, kiddo.' She hugged him tight, inhaling his
lovely little-boy scent. 'What are you drawing?'

He wriggled out of her hold, grabbed the board
and held it up.

She smiled. 'Is that a picture of Mister Pickles?'

He nodded. 'I miss him.'

'Me, too. But you know Chloe's taking good care
of him, right?'

'Yeah.' His face brightened. 'Are we going to the
beach today?'

She hesitated. 'Maybe,' she said, even as she
thought of the note she'd yet to read and felt her
heart sink. Why would Luca write her a note unless

he wasn't planning on seeing them today? To distract Ethan, she asked, 'Have you eaten some breakfast?'

He informed her that Celeste had given him some fruit and toast. He went back to his drawing, and Annah sat at the sunny table in front of the French doors overlooking the gardens. The table was laden with fruit, yoghurt, pastries, toast and spreads, a glass jug filled with orange juice, and two silver carafes, one with coffee and one with tea. It was a crazy amount of food for an adult and a child. Annah hoped what they didn't eat wouldn't go to waste.

Spotting the small envelope propped against a floral china teacup, she plucked it off the table, took a deep breath, and pulled out the note.

Luca's handwriting was large and bold.

Annah,
An urgent work matter has arisen that requires my attention. I apologise, but I cannot spend the day with you and Ethan as planned.
I will endeavour to return by early evening before he goes to bed. In the meantime, perhaps you can enjoy exploring the estate.
The staff are at your disposal.
Luca

She crumpled the note in her hand. Luca had promised their son a day at the beach and now she had to tell Ethan it wasn't happening. Her stomach balled into a hard knot of disappointment. Luca had a

lot to learn about parenting—like not making promises he couldn't keep.

Her stomach growled and she picked up a pastry
and sank her teeth into its delicious flakiness. Last
night she'd fallen asleep surprisingly quickly, but
then she'd awoken at some time after midnight, her
empty stomach churning with a nameless anxiety.

At home, she would have risen, made herself a cup
of hot milk and settled her mind by jotting down a
to-do list for the next day.

Here, she didn't even know where to find the
kitchen. And what was the point of a to-do list when
Celeste and the rest of the staff were unlikely to let
her lift a finger?

She finished off her pastry, went to shower and
dress and then broke the bad news to Ethan, assuring herself the pang of disappointment she felt was
on her son's behalf and not her own. If anything, the
less time she had to spend with Luca, the better. Pretending she wasn't attracted to him was exhausting.
It made her want to surrender and that was crazy,
dangerous thinking. Sleeping with her son's father
would only make their situation impossibly messy.

Ethan was downcast for a few minutes after she
told him, but he perked up when she suggested they
go exploring. As they ventured out, his infectious
enthusiasm lifted her mood. The grounds were vast,
with dozens of winding paths leading in different directions. The landscaped gardens with their emerald-
green lawns, ornamental hedges and neat rose bushes

were beautiful, but Annah was even more enchanted by the less manicured areas, where the flowers and shrubs grew wild and you couldn't quite tell where the path would lead you next. They spent some time at a pond counting giant goldfish, and later, as they made their way back to the villa, came across a massive swimming pool surrounded by towering palms and an inviting sundeck.

The only thing that marred the experience was the uncomfortable prickling sensation at the back of Annah's neck that came and went throughout the morning. The guards and dogs may not have been visible, but she knew they were there, watching.

Not surprisingly, Celeste pounced the instant they got back to their rooms, as if she, like the guards, was lurking in the shadows, observing Annah and Ethan's every move.

Had Luca instructed his staff to keep an eye on them?

She pushed the unsettling thought aside and responded to Celeste's offer of lunch. 'Just sandwiches, please,' she told the girl, thinking of the ridiculous mountain of food at breakfast.

An hour later, watered and fed, she and Ethan sat on the balcony off the sitting room, reading a book together. The spring day had grown warm and she'd pushed the French doors open after finally getting rid of Celeste. She could have taken Ethan back to the gardens or the swimming pool, but up here she could relax, knowing they weren't being watched.

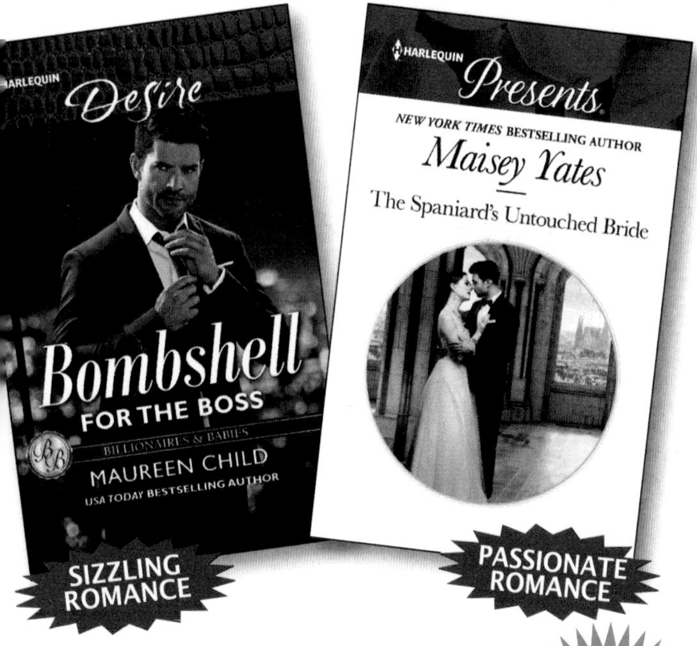

Get Up To 4 Free Books!

Dear Reader,

IT'S A FACT: if you answer 4 quick questions, we'll send you 4 FREE REWARDS from each series you try!

Try **Harlequin® Desire** books featuring heroes who have it all: wealth, status, incredible good looks...everything but the right woman.

Try **Harlequin Presents® Larger-print** books featuring a sensational and sophisticated world of international romance where sinfully tempting heroes ignite passion.

Or **TRY BOTH!**

I'm not kidding you. As a leading publisher of women's fiction, we value your opinions... and your time. That's why we are prepared to reward you handsomely for completing our mini-survey. In fact, we have 4 Free Rewards for you, including 2 free books and 2 free gifts from each series you try!

Thank you for participating in our survey,

Pam Powers

To get your 4 FREE REWARDS:
Complete the survey below and return the insert today to receive up to 4 FREE BOOKS and FREE GIFTS guaranteed!

"4 for 4" MINI-SURVEY

1 Is reading one of your favorite hobbies?
☐ YES ☐ NO

2 Do you prefer to read instead of watch TV?
☐ YES ☐ NO

3 Do you read newspapers and magazines?
☐ YES ☐ NO

4 Do you enjoy trying new book series with FREE BOOKS?
☐ YES ☐ NO

Please send me my Free Rewards, consisting of **2 Free Books from each series I select** and **Free Mystery Gifts**. I understand that I am under no obligation to buy anything, as explained on the back of this card.

❏ **Harlequin® Desire** (225/326 HDL GNW7)
❏ **Harlequin Presents® Larger-print** (176/376 HDL GNW7)
❏ **Try Both** (225/326/176/376 HDL GNML)

FIRST NAME	LAST NAME

ADDRESS

APT.#	CITY

STATE/PROV.	ZIP/POSTAL CODE

When a knock sounded on the door, she stifled a groan.

Celeste was going to drive her nuts!

She read out loud the last few words of the story, slipped Ethan off her lap, and told him to go choose another book from his bedroom. She strode to the door. 'Honestly, Celeste,' she said, reaching for the knob, 'we really don't need any—' Her voice halted the instant she opened the door and saw a woman who was not the maid. 'Oh, I—I'm sorry,' she stuttered. 'I thought you were Celeste.'

The woman blinked at her and Annah wanted to curl up and die of embarrassment because she knew at once who this was. The olive skin, dark hair, and liquid brown eyes were instant giveaways. She was an older, female version of Luca—and Ethan.

'Annah?'

'Yes.' She hesitated. 'Mrs Cavallari?'

The woman smiled. 'Yes. But call me Eva, please. I hope I'm not intruding?'

'Of course not,' Annah said quickly. 'I'm, um, sorry to have mistaken you for Celeste.'

'You're not having any problems with her, I hope?'

'Oh, no. She's been wonderful. She's just a little…'

'Eager to please?' Eva supplied.

Annah's shoulders relaxed. She gave a little laugh. 'Yes. Very.'

Eva said, 'Well, I just wanted to see that you've settled in all right—and apologise for my absence yesterday. You must have thought me terribly rude.'

Annah shook her head. 'Not at all. I'm sorry you weren't well.'

'It was just a migraine. They come and go.'

Stepping back, Annah opened the door wider and smiled. 'Would you like to meet your grandson?'

Eva's eyes suddenly glistened. She nodded. 'I would like that very much.'

Annah called to Ethan. When he emerged from the bedroom, Eva placed a trembling hand over her mouth and Annah could see she was fighting back tears. A lump rose in Annah's throat. Eva Cavallari was not the cool, aloof woman she'd expected. Meeting her grandson clearly meant a great deal to her. For the first time since their arrival, Annah felt glad that she and Ethan were here.

After the introductions, Eva invited them to join her for afternoon tea in the garden and arranged for two staff members to carry down a large wooden chest. She helped Ethan lift the lid and his eyes goggled. The chest was filled with old, beautifully preserved toys.

'These belonged to my boys,' Eva explained to Annah, a hint of melancholy in her smile. 'I could never bring myself to give them away.'

Ethan, thinking Christmas had arrived early, played happily on the lawn while his mother and grandmother sat in the shade of a gazebo.

Out of the blue, Eva said quietly, 'You must wonder what kind of woman I am to have stayed married to a man like Luca's father.'

Annah looked at her and tried to contain her surprise. 'It's really none of my business,' she said, even though the question had entered her thoughts.

Eva's lips quivered. She pressed them tightly together. After a moment, she said, 'I'm so sorry, Annah. For what Franco did. If I had known...'

Hearing the anguish in the older woman's voice, Annah reached across the table and laid her hand on Eva's. 'What's done is done,' she said gently, speaking the same words she'd repeated to herself many times in recent days. 'The best we can do now is focus on the future.'

Eva put her other hand over Annah's and offered a grateful smile. 'I wish my son were as forgiving as you, my dear.'

Annah frowned. 'He doesn't blame you for his father's actions, surely?'

Eva sat back, her gaze settling on Ethan as he ran across the lawn holding aloft a wooden toy aeroplane. 'Not for this, perhaps. But Luca has been angry with me for many years. He thinks I should have left his father and taken him and Enzo with me when they were young.' She paused, shook her head. 'Franco was not the kind of man you walk away from. He would never have let me take the boys, and I would never have left them.' She smiled sadly. 'I thought if I stayed I could protect them. In the end, in different ways, I lost them both.'

Annah's heart twisted with sympathy. 'I'm so sorry about Enzo.'

Eva looked at her in surprise. 'Luca told you?'

'Not the details. Just that his brother died three years ago.'

Eva nodded. Her gaze sought out Ethan again, as if the sight of him brought her comfort. 'Ethan looks so much like Luca and Enzo did when they were little.'

As if sensing the women's attention, Ethan turned and bounded across the grass towards them. Annah's heart swelled with love. She couldn't begin to imagine the kind of pain Eva had suffered, losing her youngest son.

Ethan leant against the side of his grandmother's chair. 'What should I call you?'

Eva bent her head down. 'Can you say *nonna*?'

'*Nonna,*' he repeated, and he and his grandmother beamed at each other.

Annah's heart gave another fierce squeeze. She thought of her own mother, who'd visited her grandson once when he was tiny and shown little interest in him. Yet here was Eva, patently thrilled to acknowledge her grandson.

Luca was right. Ethan was half-Sicilian. Half-Cavallari. Luca and Eva were his family and they wanted to be a part of his life. How could Annah deny him their love? She couldn't. No more than she could ever withhold her own love from him.

Which meant she didn't have a choice. She and Luca had to find a way to make this co-parenting thing work.

* * *

Luca prowled down the marble hallway towards the dining room, his dark, edgy mood not improved by the knowledge that his thirty-six-hour absence would not have done him any favours with Annah.

He glanced at his watch and grimaced. After not returning at all the previous night, he had called Victor and asked him to inform Annah and his mother to expect him by seven-thirty this evening at the latest.

It was now nine o'clock.

He reached the dining room and found it empty. Cursing under his breath, he spun on his heel and encountered Victor.

'Drawing room,' Victor said before Luca could open his mouth.

'Both?'

'Yes. Enjoying a *digestif*, I believe.'

Great. Two potentially unhappy women to pacify. He blew out a big breath, tempted to retire to his room and face the music tomorrow. But no. He owed Annah an explanation. And he needed to see her tonight. Reassure himself that all his efforts to earn her trust thus far hadn't been totally negated.

When he walked into the drawing room, she and his mother looked surprisingly cosy sitting on a gold velvet chesterfield sofa, large snifters of brandy on the low table in front of them. They stopped talking and looked at him. He scrutinised Annah's face, but her features were impassive, her mood impossible to read.

'I apologise for missing dinner,' he said stiffly. He crossed to the drinks cabinet and poured himself a whisky. The silence behind him spoke volumes. He turned to face them, feeling rather like a man standing in front of a firing squad. He dropped into an armchair, looked at his mother and tried for a civil tone. 'Are you feeling better?'

'Yes. Thank you.' Her gaze moved over his face for a moment. 'You look tired, Luca.'

He took a slug of whisky. He *was* tired. Exhausted, in fact. He and Mario had spent thirty-plus hours orchestrating a sting operation to catch an employee fencing stolen goods through one of the company's warehouses—exactly the kind of illegal activity he was determined to stamp out. Several more hours had been devoted to dealing with the authorities and their endless layers of bureaucracy.

But suddenly all of that seemed like too much to explain. 'I've been working,' he said succinctly.

'I realise. But must you work so hard?'

His temper snapped. She knew why he worked the hours he did. Because his father—*her* husband whose side she'd stood by for over thirty years—had left behind a godawful mess that Luca was trying his damnedest to clean up. 'Your concern for my welfare is about twenty years too late, Mother.'

Annah gasped. 'Luca!'

It was the first thing she'd said since he'd walked into the room, and the reproach in her tone darkened his mood further.

Dammit. He didn't want her seeing him like this, at his worst. This had been a mistake. He knocked back his whisky, snapped his tumbler onto the table, and stood. 'Forgive me. I'm clearly not in a socialising mood.'

He stalked out of the room and started up the stairs.

'Luca.'

Annah's voice floated up to him. Abruptly, he stopped and turned. She walked up, pausing two steps below him, and he let his gaze travel down her body and up again. In white jeans and a simple applegreen top, she looked beautiful and fresh—the perfect counterpoint to all the ugliness he'd dealt with over the past thirty-six hours. Since he'd last seen her she'd caught the sun. Or maybe the brandy had put the glow in her cheeks.

A kick of lust lent his mood a dangerous edge. 'Leave me,' he growled. 'I'm not the best company right now.' He turned his back on her and continued up the stairs, hoping she had the sense to heed his warning.

'Luca.'

He discerned frustration in her voice. And hurt. Tamping down his guilt, he strode past the study and on to his room. If she had any sense of self-preservation, she'd know better than to follow him into any room that contained a bed. He shoved the door open, flipped on the light, and swung around, forcing her to slam to a stop in front of him.

Panting a little, she stood on the threshold and glared. 'Don't you dare shut that door in my face.'

He flared his nostrils. *Shut the door*, a voice in his head commanded. But it was too late. The devil was already rising in him. He stood back and motioned her into the room with a flourish of his hand. 'Be my guest.'

She walked past him, then stopped in mid-stride.

Luca raised an eyebrow. 'Changed your mind?'

She swung around to face him, turning away from his massive four-poster bed. Her cheeks glowed bright pink. 'Isn't there somewhere else we can talk?'

'I'm not in a talking mood.' He trailed his gaze slowly over her figure, deliberately stoking his hunger so it would show on his face—a fair warning to her to get the hell out while she still had the chance.

She didn't budge.

'Last chance, *cara*,' he said in a low voice, his hand braced on the edge of the door. 'Staying or going?'

CHAPTER SEVEN

ANNAH STOOD HER ground despite the jittery sensation in the pit of her stomach and the inner voice warning her to flee.

Luca's eyes might be glittering with wolfish intent, but he wasn't going to do anything. Not with his son sleeping down the hall and his mother downstairs. This was just a scare tactic to avoid a conversation he didn't want to have.

She crossed her arms over her chest. 'I'm not going until we've talked,' she said, putting a slight emphasis on the word *talked* in case he mistakenly thought she had other ideas.

He shrugged. 'Suit yourself.'

And then he closed the door and crossed to another, leaving her to follow.

Annah felt a ping of relief. Like the guest bedroom, this room probably had an adjoining sitting room. Somewhere they could sit and have a conversation. She wanted to know why he'd spoken to his mother the way he had. She still had a lot to learn about Luca, but she didn't believe he was a cruel man. Neither did she believe he would cancel his plans to spend time with their son without good reason. But she couldn't excuse his absence, or his behaviour, unless she understood what was going on with him.

He pushed open the door, and she followed him into the next room and then stopped short. It wasn't a sitting room. It was the biggest walk-in wardrobe she'd ever seen. So big there was even an island in the centre populated with drawers and cubby holes stacked with shoes and neatly folded clothes. She lifted her gaze and blinked at long rows of hanging designer suits and shirts.

'I thought you wanted to talk.'

Luca's dry-voiced remark jerked her attention back to him. She hovered uncertainly against the wall, close to the doorway, and tried to stop her eyes from widening as Luca began to unbutton his shirt.

She swallowed and then cleared her throat. 'Why did you say something so hurtful to your mother?'

He paused on the last button and looked up. 'I am not having a discussion with you about my mother,' he said flatly. And then he peeled off his shirt and tossed it into a laundry basket.

Annah pressed her palms against the wall behind her and tried to control where she looked, but her eyes slid helplessly downwards, roving over powerful shoulders, strong arms, and a broad chest that was a true masterpiece of hard muscle and taut skin with a fine dusting of dark hair over impressive pecs.

A wave of heat crashed through her. She forced her eyes up. He was watching her and she suddenly felt exposed, as if he could see on her face just how badly she wanted him. He moved towards her, his dark eyes burning into hers until she felt the heat sizzling all the way down to her pelvis.

He planted his hand on the wall beside her head, between her and the doorway. With lazy movements, he lifted his other hand and wound a tendril of her hair around his forefinger. 'Do you ever think about that night in London?' he murmured.

She thought about saying no, but he'd know she was lying. 'Yes,' she admitted after a moment. 'Do you?'

'More often than you can imagine.'

His answer made her heart stutter. She sucked in a breath. This was dangerous. Reckless. Like playing with fire and hoping she wouldn't get burnt. 'I... I should go,' she croaked.

'Is that what you want?' he challenged in a husky voice.

She pushed her head back against the wall. He was so close she could angle her chin and press her mouth against his throat if she wanted to. All these years later, she still remembered how it felt to kiss his skin. The heat of him against her lips. What it was like to explore his body with her unskilled mouth and make him shudder and groan. A longing rose, so powerful it made her chest ache. Her clitoris throb. 'No,' she whispered. 'It's not what I want.'

His eyes smouldered and then he pulled her against him and captured her mouth in a hot, urgent kiss.

Annah's insides caught fire. Leaning into him, she kissed him back and let her hands slide over his shoulders and torso, relishing his taste and the delicious feel of smooth skin over hard, powerful muscle.

God, how she wanted him.

And if the hard ridge pressing against her belly was any indication, he wanted her just as much.

The knowledge intensified the ache between her thighs, and a little whimper of need climbed her throat. As if he understood, his hands went to the front of her jeans and deftly undid them. When he slipped one hand inside her knickers, she gasped against his mouth.

'I've dreamed of touching you like this,' he said roughly, his fingers stroking between her sensitive folds while his lips trailed across her jaw and down her neck. 'Do you remember how it was, *cara*?' he growled against her throat. 'How good we were together? How you came apart in my arms?'

'Yes,' she breathed, clutching his shoulders, gasping her pleasure as she writhed against his hand and shamelessly pushed her most sensitive part against his palm. It didn't take much more—only the slide of his fingers inside her—to have her climaxing in a hot, wet rush.

A low moan poured from her throat, matched by a deep growl of satisfaction from Luca.

And then their mouths melded again, their kissing growing more heated, more frantic. Luca pushed her top up, freed one of her breasts from its lace cup, then dipped his head and covered her already taut nipple with his mouth.

Annah gasped, the hot wire of need tightening at her core again. Her hands went to the waistband of his trousers, fingers fumbling as she worked at the belt and zipper and then finally freed his glorious erection. She closed her hand around the silken length and he sucked in his breath.

'I want this inside me,' she whispered boldly.

It was all the encouragement he needed. With a few swift movements he yanked off her knickers and jeans, getting rid of her shoes at the same time, then dispensed with the rest of his own clothing. After reaching into a drawer, he sheathed himself with a condom and then lifted her up as if she weighed nothing.

Annah wrapped her arms and legs around him as he thrust into her, driving deep, and it seemed as if her body and soul gasped in unison. It felt so right, so perfect, as if he were the only man who could ever make her feel this wonderful.

He kissed her, their tongues entwining as he pounded into her and they came together, a great shudder racking Luca's powerful body. Annah clung to him, shivery aftershocks pulsing through her limbs, and he held her against him as their heart-beats returned to normal.

'My God…' Luca's voice was hoarse. Slowly, he withdrew and Annah lowered her legs. He glanced down at his sheathed member. 'Let me take care of this,' he murmured and moved away, going to his en suite bathroom, she presumed.

Legs trembling, Annah closed her eyes and sagged against the wall, taking a moment to get her breathing under control. When she opened her eyes again, she startled at the sight of her reflection in a tall mirror on the opposite wall.

Shock reverberated down her spine. *Good God.* She looked like a wanton hussy. Top pushed up. One breast hanging out of her bra. The rest of her as naked as the day she was born.

A chill scuttled over her skin.

What was she doing?

Behaving like a trollop while her little boy slept at the other end of the hallway, that was what!

Hastily, she sorted out her bra and top and then pulled on her knickers and jeans.

'Annah?'

She straightened at the sound of Luca's voice, a mix of desire and dismay streaking through her when she saw he was still naked. She tried hard not to look at his beautiful body. 'I think I should go,' she croaked and, giving him no chance to respond, grabbed her shoes and fled, praying she wouldn't run into Celeste or Victor or—heaven forbid—Eva on the way back to her room.

The next morning, Luca cleared his schedule for the next seventy-two hours. He had a fair bit of making up to do. Not only to Ethan for breaking his promise, but to Annah after his appalling behaviour last night. Self-disgust rattled in him. All the times over the years he'd imagined having her again, and when the opportunity finally came, what did he do? Took her up against the wall of his wardrobe with an utter lack of finesse. Was it any wonder she'd fled?

And yet, incredibly, a silver lining had emerged. A startling moment of clarity that struck as he stood on his moonlit balcony, staring out at the land his son would one day inherit.

A son who did not even bear the Cavallari name.

A son whose parents would bandy him back and forth like a ping-pong ball between England and Sicily for the next fourteen years.

It was unacceptable.

Yet he'd been at such pains to show Annah he was a reasonable man and nothing like his father, he'd ended up willing to compromise and, in the process, short-change his own son.

The answer was so obvious Luca didn't know why it hadn't occurred to him before last night.

He and Annah would marry. It was the perfect solution. Already they were united by their common goal to protect and provide for their son. Formalising their partnership into a legal, permanent arrangement was simply a logical next step. And their marriage would not be a passionless one. Far from it. Their chemistry was blisteringly hot. Last night had proven that. He couldn't imagine their attraction ever waning.

His resolve solidified as he sat at the round marble-top table in the sunny warmth of the breakfast room, waiting to see if the invitation he'd extended to Annah and Ethan via Celeste to join him for breakfast would be accepted or rejected. When the two of them finally appeared, relief surged. He rose to his feet as Ethan rushed over, grinning.

'Hello, Papà.'

Luca blinked, something swelling in his chest—an emotion he couldn't quite identify—at hearing his son address him for the first time as 'Papà'.

'Ciao, figlio mio,' he said, reaching down, surprised at how natural it felt to lift his child and hold him. He transferred his gaze to Annah and found her watching them, an indecipherable look on her face.

He took in her appearance with an appreciative eye. She wore a soft, cornflower-blue cardigan that matched her eyes, stretchy denim capris, and a pair of cute white espadrilles on her feet. Marvelling at how she made simple clothing look sexy, he brought his gaze back to her face. 'Good morning,' he said, noticing her cheeks had flushed a charming pink.

'Morning,' she returned, offering a quick smile before her gaze skated away and she sat at the table.

His conscience sustaining another prick of regret over last night, Luca lowered Ethan into a chair beside his mother, where he stayed for all of thirty seconds before leaping off.

'Nonna!' he exclaimed, rushing over to greet his grandmother, who'd just entered the room.

Luca put down his coffee and said quietly to Annah, 'I invited my mother to join us for breakfast. I hope you don't mind.'

She looked at him, her expression softening as he had hoped it might. 'Of course not,' she said. 'That was thoughtful.'

Ethan tugged Eva by the hand and made her sit next to him at the table.

Observing them, Luca grew aware of an odd pang in his chest. Clearly, grandmother and grandson had bonded in his absence. Lifting his cup, he took a mouthful of espresso and told himself it was foolish to feel jealous.

Annah, who had started pouring orange juice for herself and Ethan, offered one to Eva.

'*Grazie*, dear.' Eva glanced between Luca and Annah. 'And what plans do you have for today?'

'I'm taking Annah and Ethan sightseeing,' Luca said.

Annah looked at him in surprise. 'You are?'

'That sounds lovely,' said Eva.

'Yay!' Ethan chipped in. 'Are you coming, Nonna?'

Eva smiled and, much to Luca's relief, shook her head. 'Oh, no. I have some things to do today. But you can tell me all about your day when you get back.'

Over the next half-hour Luca happily discovered that a man was required to say very little in the presence of two women and a talkative child. Coffee in hand, he sat back and listened to Annah and his mother discuss pruning methods, of all things, while his gaze lingered almost exclusively on Annah.

Luca had not lived like a monk these past five years. Building his business in New York had taken priority over everything else, but he had not denied himself the company of women when he desired it.

But no other woman had fired his blood the way Annah did. None had left a permanent imprint on his memory—on his very soul—like she had. The fact that she'd borne his son only made her more desirable. He wanted her in his bed, but he wanted so much more. He wanted to give her his name. His protection. His loyalty.

The more he thought about it, the more certain he grew that marriage was the only sensible solution. The only desirable solution.

Annah belonged here, with him, as much as Ethan did.

All he had to do was convince her.

Palermo was a vibrant, chaotic city that couldn't have been further removed from the peace and quiet of Hollyfield. Having not lived in a big city for nearly five years, Annah had got used to the slower pace of the countryside and no longer thought of herself as a city lover, yet she quickly found herself entranced by Sicily's capital.

To her delight, Luca had instructed his driver to drop them in the heart of the city so they could tour its historic centre on foot.

'So many different kinds of architecture,' she remarked, stopping to stare up at a row of three Arabic domes atop an ancient stone church.

Luca looked down at her, rakishly handsome today with his stubble-darkened jaw and sexily ruffled hair. He wore snug-fitting jeans that hugged his powerful thighs, a light grey polo shirt, and designer sunglasses on his face.

He was a walking hazard.

Annah had seen four women trip over their feet while angling for a better look, and one who'd walked straight into a parked moped. Mario had rushed forward from his ever-present position at their rear to help the poor woman; Luca, who at the time was pointing something out to Ethan, was oblivious.

'Palermo has been invaded more times than any other city in the Mediterranean,' he told her. 'Romans, Arabs, Normans, the Spanish and many others—they came, conquered, and left their mark.'

Much like he'd left his mark on her last night, she thought, because no matter how hard she tried she couldn't forget the glorious feeling of his big body caging hers and the powerful thrust of his hard, hot length inside her. He'd filled her so perfectly, so completely, that when he'd withdrawn she'd felt as if he had taken a piece of her with him.

She cleared her throat. 'Fascinating,' she murmured, forcing herself to look away before her eyes betrayed her.

If Luca was having similar troubles forgetting last night's encounter, it didn't show. He'd been surprisingly relaxed and charming all morning, even inviting Eva to join them for a family breakfast.

Annah's heart flip-flopped. Family. Something Ethan had never experienced outside the two-person unit that was him and her. Sitting in the warm, sunny breakfast room, Annah had found herself picturing the table surrounded by happy, noisy children—a brood of little brothers and sisters for Ethan—before she'd yanked her mind back from such a fanciful daydream.

The morning continued to warm up as they walked, the early spring weather milder here than at home where some days still had a wintry nip. The maze of narrow streets teemed with restaurants and al fresco bars and a delightful assortment of artisan boutiques selling everything from hand-crafted leather goods and jewellery to handmade chocolates.

It wasn't all beautiful. The old town was full of baroque *palazzi*—centuries-old palaces built and owned by the Italian aristocracy—some of which stood crumbling and neglected, abandoned and left to ruin or turned into scruffy, overcrowded tenements. But many others retained their original grandeur and were still lived in by their wealthy owners.

The poignant contrast between decadence and decay gave the city a sensual, edgy vibe that seemed to infiltrate Annah's blood, so that when they came upon a boisterous street market and Luca hoisted Ethan onto his shoulders and then clasped her hand, she didn't pull away. Instead, she returned his grip and allowed herself to enjoy the contact and the resulting shimmer of heat through her body.

Some of the market's stallholders were winding down, but others still hawked their wares, shouting over the heads of the crowd. She glanced up at Ethan, worried he might find the noise and the pungent smells of seafood and meats and exotic spices overwhelming. But a wide grin split his face. He was king of the castle, riding high on his father's shoulders. He looked as happy as she'd ever seen him, and a pang of something she couldn't quite identify pierced her chest.

As they neared a fruit and vegetable stall, a short, balding man came out from beneath his awning, beaming at Luca, who released her hand to shake the man's. Annah couldn't understand the exchange that followed, but she saw how the man's eyes lit with interest on Ethan, and then her.

Luca reclaimed her hand and said, 'This is Guido. He doesn't speak English, but he is very happy to meet you.'

'Oh.' Annah sent the man a friendly smile, and

he doffed his *coppola* and grinned back, then said something to Luca.

Luca released a deep baritone laugh before responding.

'What did he say?' Annah asked as they waved goodbye and moved off.

His dark eyes gleamed with humour and something else that defied interpretation. 'He said you are very beautiful.'

'Oh!' Annah's face heated.

'And…' Luca leaned close and dropped his voice so Ethan wouldn't hear '…that if I do not plan to make an honest woman of you, he has many strapping sons he can introduce you to.'

Annah's blush intensified. She covered her embarrassment with a little laugh, wishing she had the courage to ask Luca how he'd responded. Instead, she said, 'Was that Sicilian you were speaking?'

'Yes.'

'Is it quite different from Italian?'

He nodded. 'My mother is from Naples and speaks only Italian and cannot understand Sicilian.'

'She never learned?'

He shrugged. 'There was no need.'

'But you learned both,' she observed.

'Yes. My father insisted. Both Enzo and I were fluent in both languages from a young age.'

Annah discerned a hint of tension in his voice at the mention of his brother, and she stifled the urge to pepper him with more questions. The last thing she wanted was to shatter this good mood of his. She focused instead on the bustling market around them, soaking up its lively, colourful atmosphere.

By the time they stepped inside a quaint trattoria for lunch, her feet cried out for a rest. But she'd loved every minute of exploring the old city on foot. Better than being ferried from place to place in the SUV.

The trattoria was run by an older couple who greeted them effusively and seemed especially happy to see Luca. During the introductions, Annah learnt the couple was Mario's in-laws. Mario himself had disappeared, she realised. Moments later, he emerged from the rear of the restaurant with a pretty dark-haired woman and an adorable little girl about Ethan's age. Liliana, Annah guessed, even before her proud *papà* introduced her.

'And this is my wife, Mia,' said Mario.

Mia was warm and friendly, her English better than her parents', who, like Guido at the market, were fluent only in Sicilian. She led Luca, Ethan, and Annah to a table in a lovely open courtyard and then served them refreshing lemon *granita* and mouth-watering pizza.

When they'd finished eating, Luca reached for her hand over the table. 'I need to talk with Mario and his father-in-law.' His thumb stroked lightly across her knuckles. 'I won't be long. Are you happy here for a bit?'

Sensation tingled in her hand from where his thumb stroked, but she met his eyes and told herself for the umpteenth time she was reading too much into his touch. Seeing a depth of intimacy in his dark eyes that wasn't really there. She smiled. 'Of course.'

A short while later, from where she sat, Annah could just see the three men, plus a fourth she hadn't met, huddled at a corner table inside the trattoria. 'They look serious,' she said to Mia, who'd come out to join her after Luca left. Ethan and Liliana sat at a separate table, playing with crayons and colouring books and chatting adorably.

Mia sipped her melon *granita* and nodded. 'The man next to Mario,' she said. 'He is my father's cousin, Pietro. He runs a dry-cleaning shop.' She put down her glass. 'It was firebombed six weeks ago.'

Annah gasped. 'By vandals?'

'By the people Pietro refuses to pay protection money to.'

Shock felt like an electric jolt in her chest. 'That's terrible,' she whispered.

Mia shrugged. 'It happens,' she said, but her chin went up and something like pride or defiance glowed in her brown eyes. 'But things are slowly changing here. People are standing up—taking back our city.' She flashed Annah a smile. 'Luca has been amazing. When his father died and he came back, people held their breaths, not knowing what to expect. But he is a good man. He paid for Pietro's shop renovation. And he subsidises a private security service so local businesses can afford to have their premises monitored.' She gestured with her chin to the men indoors. 'My

Mario—he would protect Luca with his life the same as he would protect Liliana and me.'

Annah's heart thudded as she tried to absorb it all. 'Doesn't it frighten you? That Mario could end up in harm's way?'

Maria shook her head. 'I do not worry. The whole world is dangerous, yes? Too many terrorists and people who are loco.' She circled her fingertip at her temple. 'But there are good men like ours fighting to make our world a safer, better place. That makes me proud, not afraid.' She reached over suddenly and squeezed Annah's hand. 'Look at our men.'

Annah's gaze fell on Luca. Even sitting down he looked solid and powerful, his chiselled features stamped with intelligence and authority.

'They are strong,' Mia said. 'Powerful. And they are Sicilian—family is *everything*.' Her hand squeezed again. 'With Luca, you and your son will always be safe.'

CHAPTER EIGHT

ANNAH LEANED OVER the bed, pulled the sheet up to Ethan's chin and gently kissed his forehead. He didn't stir, having fallen asleep within seconds of his head hitting the pillow.

Straightening, she stared down at him and pressed her hand to her throat, her emotions tumbling and swirling like fallen leaves caught on a gust of wind.

Her son's father was a good man. Annah couldn't deny that simple truth. Not after today. After hearing the things Mia had told her. After watching Luca spend time with their son. He was so determined to be a father to Ethan—a real, hands-on father, not just a wealthy man doling out child support from afar.

It filled her with a cautious sense of joy, yet tore her to bits at the same time. Luca had missed *four* years of his son's life while Ethan had been deprived of his father. It was so unfair. She almost wished Franco Cavallari were alive so she could demand to know why he had done what he had.

With a deep breath to steady her emotions, she

crept out of the bedroom, slipped her feet into high-heeled sandals, and smoothed her hands down the front of her black trousers. Her first night here she'd teamed the trousers with a black top and worn her hair in a severe style. Tonight, her top was a shimmer of turquoise silk and her hair fell in shining waves to her shoulders.

She stopped in front of the antique gold-framed wall mirror and studied her face. Did she look different? She felt different. Restless and achy in a way that wasn't anything to do with tired muscles.

So much about today had deeply moved her. The city, its history, its people. *Luca.* Even now her heart pounded as she thought of her conversation with Mia. Of the pride and respect in the young woman's voice as she'd spoken of the men and their stand against corruption. Her fearlessness and utter faith in Mario to keep her and Liliana safe—and her stout belief that Luca would do the same for Annah and Ethan.

A belief Annah realised she shared. Not once today had she worried for her and Ethan's safety. Luca's solid, indomitable presence, the gentle strength of his hand around hers, had not only warmed her soul but engendered a sense of comfort and security she'd never experienced before, even as a child.

Especially as a child.

She touched her fingers to her mouth, her skin tingling at the memory of last night's heated kiss and their urgent, explosive coupling.

Suddenly she understood this restless, achy feeling. Her body was in a state of craving. Crying out to be touched, aching to be filled by the only man she had ever desired.

Abruptly, she pulled her hand down and turned away from the mirror. She needed to focus on Ethan, on what was best for him, not on herself and her own selfish desires.

Downstairs, in the elegant sitting room where she'd sat with Eva last night, Luca and a glass of brandy awaited her.

'Thank you,' she said, accepting the crystal tumbler from him, the glint of appreciation in his dark eyes as he surveyed her appearance not escaping her notice. Neither did the fact that he'd shaved or that his hair was damp from a shower—or that he looked stunningly handsome in a pale blue open-necked shirt and charcoal trousers.

Deliberately, she turned her gaze to the open French doors, ignoring the dip and sway of her belly.

'The night is cool,' he said, following the direction of her gaze. 'But it's pleasant on the terrace with the gas heaters on if you'd like to sit outside?'

She nodded and moved towards the doors, hoping the heaters weren't *too* warm. A little crisp air to cool her libido might be a good thing. She settled against the cushions of a wicker chair while Luca lowered his large frame into the one adjacent.

His gaze settled on her. 'Did Ethan go to sleep all right?'

'Yes. Out like a light.'

After lunch, Ethan had finally got his wish to visit the beach. Luca's driver had taken them to Mondello, a small seaside resort close to the city. The beach itself was a long, curving strip of soft white sand sloping gently into clear aquamarine waters.

'In summer it's packed and not so pleasant,' Luca had said. 'But the water won't get warm enough for swimming for another month.'

Ethan still would have gone in if she'd let him, but he'd settled for paddling in the shallows and playing in the sand. Later, at the villa, Eva joined them for an early supper while Luca caught up on some work. Still buzzing, Ethan had regaled his grandmother with a long-winded account of his day.

Annah looked at Luca. 'Thank you for today,' she said softly. 'He had a wonderful time.'

Their gazes held for a long moment and then suddenly, without warning, and for no reason Annah could pinpoint, tears filled her eyes. Feeling stupid, she put her glass down, got up and walked to the edge of the terrace where the pool of light from the outdoor lamps met the darkness.

'Annah.'

Luca's voice, so bone-meltingly rich and deep, came from behind her. His hands wrapped around her upper arms and eased her back against his hard body, reminding her of the night at Fendalton Hall when she'd stalked away from the dinner table and he'd come after her—and then kissed her. She'd wanted him then and she wanted him now, more than ever.

'*Cara.*' His big hands stroked up and down her arms. 'What is it?'

Angry at herself, she blinked away her tears. Why was she so emotional? She inhaled deeply, catching the soothing scents of rosemary and jasmine from the gardens below—and a hint of spicy cologne from the man behind her.

'I'm sorry,' she said quietly. 'I just… I can't stop thinking how unfair it is that you and Ethan missed out on four years of knowing each other.' She turned in his arms and looked up at him. 'How could your father have done that to you? Luca, he told me to have an *abortion*—to get rid of his own grandchild.' She shook her head, her horror and disbelief as fresh and heart-wrenching as if she'd squared off with Franco Cavallari only yesterday. 'Why?' she said, her eyes searching his. 'Help me understand why our son spent the first four years of his life not knowing his father.'

Something bleak moved through Luca's eyes. Something that made Annah shiver.

'Come back to the warmth,' he said, drawing her by the hand to a wicker sofa instead of the chairs.

They sat on the cushions, their bodies angled towards each other. Luca's arm stretched along the top of the sofa, his hand close to Annah's shoulder.

'I was sixteen when I learnt what my father was truly capable of,' he said, his voice gruff but controlled. 'It was the worst moment of my life up until then. It turned everything I thought I knew about him into a lie and yet… I couldn't accept it. Couldn't believe the man I'd idolised as a boy existed only in my head.'

His lips twisted into a bitter smile. 'I was naive enough—and arrogant enough—to believe I could change him, turn him into the man I wanted him to be. I went to university in the States then came back and joined the family business, thinking I'd convince him to legitimise our operations.'

Annah waited, her heart clenching in her chest because she knew there was no happy ending to this story.

'I actually thought I was succeeding.' His short bark of laughter was devoid of humour. 'But Franco played me. Sent me to London to acquire and manage a transport company. Let me think he was cleaning up his act, turning over a new leaf. But the drugs, the money laundering… He never intended to stop.'

Luca moved his hand along the top of the sofa and gently caught a tendril of her hair between his fingers. 'I finally confronted him a few days before I met you. Franco was livid when I threatened to walk. Said I'd never be welcomed back.' He paused, gaze fixed on his fingers as he toyed absently with her hair. 'It was the last time we ever spoke to each other.'

Annah thought back to that night in London, recalling the glimpses of something darker beneath the surface of Luca's charm. No wonder.

He carried on. 'Perhaps sending you away was my father's idea of revenge.' He shook his head, his eyes meeting hers, something stark and desolate in them. 'You should never have had to face him. I should have considered the possibility of consequences, given you a contact number—'

Annah laid her fingers against his lips. 'Don't,' she said, and all the tumbling, twisting emotions she couldn't get a handle on today suddenly flooded into her chest and made her heart hurt unbearably. Her eyes prickled again, and she didn't blink fast enough this time; tears escaped, one from each eye, the drops hovering on her lashes for a second before trickling down her cheeks.

Luca's arms came around her and she didn't resist; it felt too good. She pressed her face against his shoulder, letting his warmth and scent envelop her, accepting comfort. *Just for a moment.* 'I'm sorry,' she said, her voice muffled against his tear-dampened shirt. 'I don't know why I'm so emotional.'

He eased her back, framed her face with his hands, and brushed his thumbs across her wet cheeks. With astonishing tenderness he kissed her forehead, and then his hands slid to her shoulders as if to gently set her away.

Everything in her protested. 'No,' she whispered, her hand tangling in the front of his shirt, her gaze dropping to his mouth.

Awareness sizzled in the air.

'Annah.' Her name was a deep rasp in his throat.

She lifted her eyes back to his, saw they were dark and molten. Emboldened by the desire she saw there, she let her hand slide to the front of his trousers and found him gratifyingly hard. She cupped him and heard his breath hiss between his teeth. 'You want me,' she said huskily.

His jaw was rigid. 'You're upset. Vulnerable. I won't take advan—'

Annah brought her mouth to his, silencing his chivalrous protest.

For long, excruciating seconds, nothing happened. A silent plea rang in her head. *Kiss me back!*

Finally, a low groan rose up his throat, and then he dragged her against the hard heat of his body and moved his mouth against hers. Relief flickered, followed by a surge of excitement, a wave of heat and need that sent her pulse rate into the stratosphere.

His tongue stroked along the seam of her lips and they parted willingly, inviting him to delve deeper. Annah tasted coffee and whisky and something salty—the residue of her tears, perhaps. She wound her arms around his neck, pressing closer, her insides melting beneath a blaze of longing.

When Luca drew back, she actually whimpered. He looked straight into her eyes. 'Are you sure?'

'Yes,' she said adamantly.

Eyes glittering, he stood and lifted her, one arm around her back, the other under her knees, and carried her inside, up the sweeping staircase and into his bedroom.

* * *

Luca set Annah on her feet next to his bed, sliding her body slowly down his, letting the brush of her soft curves against him inflame his desire.

His muscles trembled with the effort of holding himself in check.

There would be no repeat of last night. He would control his tumultuous need and make love to her slowly, attentively, with all the care the mother of his child deserved.

Tangling his hands in her golden hair, he tilted her face up and kissed her slowly, deeply, sampling her sweetness with his tongue, reacquainting himself with the shape and texture of her soft, plump lips.

His blood thrummed.

Annah wanted this, had initiated it and persisted even when he'd offered her the chance to change her mind. She might not realise it yet, but this acknowledgement of their chemistry—her willingness to surrender to it—was her first step towards reaching the same conclusion he had. That marriage would offer them not only a logical, practical solution but an eminently enjoyable one rich with its own rewards and pleasures.

He ran his hands down her back, gripped the bottom of her silky top, and whispered against her lips, 'Lift your arms, *cara*.'

She complied and he lifted the top up and over her head, throwing it onto a soft chair in the corner of the room.

One at a time, he slipped the straps of her bra down her arms, pressing an open-mouthed kiss to each bare shoulder as he went. Reaching around her, he undid the clasp, tugged the bra down and off, and sent it in the same direction as her top.

He stood back and let his eyes devour those beautiful breasts.

'Magnifico,' he murmured.

Annah's expression turned shy. Lifting her arms, she began to cover herself. But Luca stopped her, holding her wrists and spreading her arms wide.

'Let me see you,' he said and cupped his hand under one breast, savouring its softness and weight against his palm before dipping his head and sucking the tightly budded nipple into his mouth.

She shivered and made a low, breathy sound of pleasure that fired a pulse of heat directly into his groin.

Forcing himself to go slowly, he knelt and removed her shoes, trying not to tickle the sensitive arches of her feet. He unzipped her trousers and eased them down, removing her knickers at the same time.

When she stood before him naked, he leaned back on his haunches and ran his gaze appreciatively up her body, taking in the long lines of her legs, the graceful curves of her hips, and the neat thatch of golden curls at her centre. Higher up, her breasts rose and fell rapidly, as if she were out of breath and struggling to get enough air into her lungs.

Luca palmed her hips and brought his mouth to the soft, smooth skin just below her navel, a sense of wonder enveloping him as he pressed his lips to the place where she had been round with his child.

What had pregnancy been like for her? Had she suffered with morning sickness? Had she craved unusual foods? Had she laboured long and hard to bring their son into the world?

There was so much he didn't know. So much he had missed out on.

'Luca?' she said, her voice soft, uncertain.

He rose to his feet and kissed her until she trembled in his arms, and then he lifted her onto the bed, laying her across its width and tugging her hips to the edge of the mattress.

His heart pounded unevenly, as if he were an unfledged youth making love to a woman for the first time in his life.

Crazy.

Why did she affect him like this?

He no more knew the answer now than he had five years ago in London.

Dropping to his knees on the floor, he parted her legs and heard her suck in her breath as he hooked them over his shoulders and kissed his way down the silken length of one inner thigh. When he reached his destination, he stroked his fingertips through soft, golden curls and into folds already swollen and slick with arousal. He inhaled, dragging the scent of her delicate musk into his lungs, and then he tasted, running his tongue along that seam of hot, feminine flesh.

'Oh…' She groaned, her hips bucking and lifting until Luca splayed his hand across her stomach, anchoring her to the bed.

He pushed his finger inside her, amazed at how tight she was. How ready. One more hot glide of his tongue in the right spot and—

Her fingers plunged into his hair and she cried out as her internal muscles clenched hard and then rippled around his finger.

Annah's body went limp, but little gasped moans continued to rise from her throat.

Luca's blood roared with satisfaction. Easing his shoulders out from under her legs, he trailed kisses up her body, pausing to circle his tongue around her navel then to lavish attention on her breasts before finally taking possession of her mouth.

'Take me,' she whispered against his lips, and those husky words almost had him spilling inside his boxers.

He pushed off the bed, stripped off his clothes, and sheathed himself with a condom. He could hear nothing but the thud of his pulse and the rasp of his breathing as he joined Annah on the bed again.

With a single, sure stroke he sank deep into her velvety heat, the sheer ecstasy of their bodies joining as one pushing a massive, shuddering sigh from the depths of his chest. Her long legs circled his hips and her hands gripped his shoulders, her beautiful body trembling and bowing beneath him as he rode them both towards climax.

His heart thundered as white-hot sensation ripped through his centre.

Annah clung to him, a sob wrenching from her throat as they careened over the edge together.

Perfect.

The word pulsed in Luca's head as he rolled onto his back and took her with him, holding her close as aftershocks continued to quake through their bodies.

They were perfect together.

Why would he ever want another woman when he could have Annah? The mother of his child. Mother to many more of his children if he got his way.

A fierce swell of unfamiliar emotion surged in his chest. For a moment he felt intensely discomfited, until he recognised the emotions for what they were.

Possessiveness.

Protectiveness.

It made sense he would feel those things. Annah and Ethan were his family. A man was bound by honour and duty to protect his family. It was the Sicilian way.

He stroked a possessive hand over Annah's hip. Protecting her and their son would be a damned sight easier once they carried his name. His resolve strengthened. Binding them to him was the only acceptable solution.

Annah would become his wife.

Sooner rather than later.

* * *

Annah awoke with a violent start and sat bolt upright. She blinked rapidly, her heart rate galloping, her breathing fast and uneven. Her body ached in strange places and her mouth was so dry each gulp of air scraped her throat like a razor.

Where was she?

Ethan.

Blindly, she threw off the covers, stumbled to her feet and walked straight into a wall. A rather odd wall, for it radiated heat and somehow she bounced right off it.

'Annah.'

A man's voice. A voice she still recognised after all these years. A voice that should have terrified but soothed instead with its deep, measured cadence.

'Wake up.'

Oh, God. It was definitely him. She would never forget that seductive baritone—or the wicked things he had done to her body. She threw a panicked look over her shoulder. Why couldn't she see him? And why was he telling her to wake up? What did he want?

No…

Ethan.

She sucked in her breath, opened her mouth to scream, but the wall of heat suddenly engulfed her and then something hot and firm covered her mouth.

For a moment, a sense of comfort and security enveloped her like a cosy blanket. Then her body stirred in those strange places where she ached, tiny pings of sensation darting along her nerve endings.

Annah came fully awake. She stood beside the bed, held up by strong arms, her breasts squished against the hot, hard planes of a muscular chest.

Luca's mouth was on hers, and she was kissing him back.

A sound of surprise squeaked in her throat.

He lifted his head. His gaze locked on hers, eyes dark with concern. 'Are you all right?' he said after a moment.

She pulled in a shaky breath and nodded.

'You were going to scream,' he said.

She nodded again, not yet trusting her voice. He must have kissed her to silence her. *Thank heavens.* Imagine if she had screamed. Goodness knew who might have come running and discovered her here in Luca's room. Victor. Celeste. *Eva.* The very idea made her cheeks sting with mortification.

Luca stroked her hair back from her face. 'Were you sleepwalking?'

'Sort of,' she croaked. 'More a panic attack combined with not being properly awake.' She shrugged, the movement jerky. 'It's nothing. It used to happen a lot when Ethan was a baby.'

He frowned. 'Something usually triggers it?'

'Not really.' She eased away from his bare chest and noticed the drawstring pyjama bottoms riding low on his hips and, lower still, the unmistakable tenting of the cotton fabric. Her gaze darted back to his.

He shrugged, a sexy half-smile slanting his mouth. 'I've just been kissing a naked woman.'

Reminded of the fact she wore not a stitch, she clasped her arms across her front and looked at the chair on which her clothes lay. 'I should get dressed and go check on Ethan.'

'I looked in on him twenty minutes ago,' Luca said, surprising her. 'He's fine. Asleep.'

She swallowed. 'What time is it?'

'It's only midnight.' He tucked a strand of hair behind her ear. 'Wait there.' He strode off, disappeared into his enormous walk-in wardrobe, and came back with a soft towelling robe.

He held it open and she slid her arms in. 'Thank you,' she murmured, ridiculously touched by the simple gesture. She tied the robe at her waist and noticed the pool of soft lighting in a corner of the room where a lamp, a coffee table, and two upholstered chairs resided. An open laptop sat on the table. 'Were you working?' she asked.

'Just keeping on top of some things.'

She bit her lip for a second. 'I... I could go.'

In answer, Luca slipped his arm around her waist and pulled her tightly against him. 'You're not going anywhere.' His gruff statement made her body tingle with a rush of pleasure. He tipped up her chin. 'You're going to tell me about these panic attacks.'

The pleasant tingling gave way to a prickle of dismay. 'There's not much to tell.'

'It won't take long, then,' he said, his tone damp-

ening her hopes of avoiding a conversation alto-
gether. His gaze dropped to her mouth, the banked
heat in his eyes sending a shiver of secret delight
through her. 'And afterwards we will go back to bed,
yes?'

She sighed. She hated talking about herself, especially if it made her feel anything less than strong and
capable. Knowing what she'd rather do, she pouted
her mouth and trailed her fingertip through the dark
hair on his chest. 'Or we could just go straight to
bed.'

His deep, sexy chuckle made the muscles in her
pelvis contract. He removed her finger from his
chest. 'Nice try, *dolcezza*.'

She huffed out a resigned breath.

'Can I have some water, then?'

He guided her to one of the chairs, went to the en
suite and returned with a glass of water. As he lowered his tall, bare-chested frame into the other chair,
Annah quenched her thirst, then put the glass down
and tucked her feet up under her.

'Your father frightened me, Luca,' she said quietly, deciding an honest, abbreviated account was
the most painless way forward. 'I didn't know if the
things I'd heard were true, but I knew, having met
him in person, that he was not someone to cross.
After Ethan was born, I was afraid of what would
happen if your father...' She hesitated before adding, 'Or you found out I'd gone through with the
pregnancy.'

Grim lines bracketed Luca's mouth, and her heart twisted at the torment in his dark eyes. She knew it hurt him deeply that she'd once believed he'd rejected her and their unborn child and left her at his father's mercy.

'And the panic attacks?' he said.

Annah tugged the robe over her knees. 'They didn't happen often. But sometimes anxiety got the better of me. There were days when I found myself looking over my shoulder, worried someone would try to take Ethan.'

Luca's expression tightened. 'You should not have had to go through that.' Repressed anger laced his voice. He leaned forward and captured her hand. Before she realised his intent, he tugged her out of the chair and onto his lap.

She should have protested. But it felt too wonderful, being surrounded by all that heat and muscle. One large hand slipped under the robe and settled on her thigh, making her pulse thrum.

'Who supported you through your pregnancy, *cara*?'

She frowned. 'What do you mean?'

'When you were tired. Or unwell. Who did you rely on?'

He looked at her a little too intently. Did he wonder if she'd had a boyfriend? She shrugged. 'I didn't rely on anyone. But I wasn't completely alone. I had Chloe.' They'd shared the flat over the shop to begin with, right up until two years ago when Chloe had moved in with Ben.

'Your parents didn't help?'

She dropped her gaze.

'Annah?'

'No,' she said after a pause. 'My mother and I aren't close.'

'And your father?'

Her discomfort grew. 'I never knew my father,' she admitted.

'Did he die?' Luca asked gently.

Annah began to shake her head, then stopped. The truth was she didn't know if her father was dead or alive. She had no way of knowing. She took a deep breath, blew it out slowly. Luca had weathered his own discomfort last night to talk about his father. Surely she could do the same?

'I was the result of a one-night stand,' she said, staring at her hands. 'My mother was young and drunk...' She stopped herself from adding *and irresponsible*. That was one stone she couldn't cast. Not when she was guilty of the same transgression. 'Afterwards, she couldn't even remember his name or where he was from.'

She looked up, searching for signs of judgement on Luca's face, but saw none. His expression was simply intent, his gaze steady, encouraging her to go on. 'She was only nineteen when she had me and not terribly maternal—her words,' she added, 'not mine. To be honest, I don't know why she didn't give me up for adoption.'

Luca's thumb moved in soft, tantalising circles on her thigh. 'Perhaps she loved you too much to do the right thing.'

Annah stared at Luca. It was a strange thing to say. 'If she did love me, she had an odd way of showing it.'

His brow furrowed. 'How so?'

She paused, searching for the words to explain, slightly startled to realise she *wanted* to explain. 'I think I was a hindrance more than anything. At first because she was young and wanted to party. And then because she wanted a relationship and most of her boyfriends didn't want the responsibility of another man's child.'

The vertical crease between Luca's eyebrows deepened. 'Most?' he echoed. 'How many were there?'

Annah shrugged. 'I can't remember. Some weren't around for long. Some we lived with for a while.' She'd hated the constant moving. Never feeling settled. Always waiting for the day her mother would uproot them again. 'Her relationships never lasted. She was…clingy. I think she drove the men away, although…' She hesitated, old hurt rising, pulling her throat tight. 'Sometimes she told me it was my fault.'

Luca's hand stilled on her thigh. 'Tell me you didn't buy into that.'

She lifted a shoulder. 'Children tend to believe what their parents tell them.' She forced a smile. 'But, no, as an adult—and a mother—I know better.'

Moving his hand from her leg, Luca cupped the side of her face. 'You're a good mother.'

The conviction in his voice made her heart hitch. 'How do you know?' she challenged.

'Because our son is a healthy, well-rounded child,' he said. 'That is your doing, no one else's.'

Annah couldn't suppress a glow of warmth at his praise, and yet...

Wasn't she behaving just a little bit like her mother right now? Putting her own desires ahead of her child's welfare?

Unease filtered through her stomach.

She and Luca should be discussing joint custody arrangements and other matters relating to Ethan's future. Instead, they'd had sex. And now they were talking about *her*. As if her childhood mattered a jot.

Luca must have felt her stiffen. 'What?' he said.

'We need to have a conversation about custody,' she reminded him.

Something enigmatic moved through his dark gaze. 'We have the rest of the week,' he said. 'Plenty of time to talk.' His hand glided lazily down her neck, delved into the opening of the robe, and closed over her naked breast.

Annah inhaled sharply, the heat from his touch racing through her body. 'Luca,' she breathed, but her protest was husky. Half-hearted.

Dark eyes glittering, he pushed the robe open then trailed his hand between her legs, sliding his fingers through her damp heat.

She gasped, her body quickening, the exquisite ache in her pelvis intensified by the feel of his erection hardening and thickening beneath her buttocks.

Luca leaned forward, captured one of her nipples in his mouth, and sucked hard while circling her clitoris with a slick fingertip.

Annah's head fell back, her eyes closing, any thoughts of resisting swallowed by a fireball of need.

Tomorrow, she promised herself. Tomorrow they would talk.

CHAPTER NINE

OVER THE NEXT few days a deep sense of satisfaction thrummed in Luca's blood. Things were going better than he'd hoped. For three nights in a row Annah had come to his bed of her own accord, and that pleased him immensely. Yet again he'd proved to her—and himself—that he was nothing like his father. He did not bully and take what he wanted by force simply because he had the power to do so.

The more time he spent with Annah and Ethan, the stronger his conviction grew. Their son deserved a stable home with two parents united in their efforts to care and provide for him. To ferry Ethan back and forth between countries, disrupt his schooling, force him to choose which parent to spend holidays and important occasions with, was untenable.

'This view is fantastic.'

Annah sent him a beaming smile that punched the breath from his lungs. He'd seen that magnificent smile often over the last few days, but each time it still caught him like a sucker-punch.

'You think this is the right spot?' he said, genuinely interested in her thoughts on the location his winery manager had proposed for a restaurant and/or function venue.

'Yes.' She nodded enthusiastically. 'If you had big picture windows facing this way, and a landscaped outdoor area, then you'd have the view over the orchards and meadows with the sea in the distance, plus all-day sun.'

He nodded, looking across the valley. Yes. She was right about the aspect. He captured her hand and brought it to his lips. He enjoyed her like this. Smiling. Unguarded. Sexy as hell in that little lemon sundress that showed off her legs. He silently thanked the weather gods for the warm desert winds that blew in from the African continent.

They walked back down the rise and returned to the picnic blanket beneath the big spreading branches of an oak tree.

Annah leaned back on her hands. 'I loved Taormina, and I doubt Ethan will ever stop talking about the helicopter ride over Mount Etna, but I think this is my favourite place of all, right here on the estate. It's so pretty and peaceful and…' she glanced sideways at him '…there's no Mario.'

He gave her a deadpan look. 'I think Mario would be hurt to hear you say that.'

She laughed and the sound trickled through his insides like liquid honey. He held her gaze, and as their humour subsided he saw a flicker of uncertainty and conflict in her sapphire eyes. Guilt needled him. He had to concede he'd not played entirely fair these last few days. Whenever she'd grown serious or seemed about to broach a meaningful conversation, he'd deliberately distracted her.

It wasn't difficult.

She was so physically responsive to him, and he to her. A single touch could see them both consumed by fire and need.

They were careful in front of others, especially Ethan. Annah let Luca hold her hand in front of their son, but nothing more intimate. And she was gone from Luca's bedroom by five-thirty each morning, afraid Ethan might wake early and find her absent.

Luca didn't object. After hearing about her childhood, he understood her better. He'd coaxed even more from her since Tuesday, and it shredded his gut to think of her as an eight-year-old child, cooking her own dinner and sitting home alone because her mother was out with her latest boyfriend.

No wonder she was so fiercely independent.

He reached out, stroked his knuckles down her cheek. 'Tonight,' he promised, 'we'll talk.' Convincing her to relinquish some of her independence wouldn't be easy, but he was confident. Especially now she'd had a taste of the life she could have here with him, sharing his home, his bed.

She nodded, although something he couldn't identify moved across her features. Her gaze drifted to the meadow below, where Eva was showing Ethan how to fly a small kite.

'Thank you for inviting Eva to join us today,' she said.

He shrugged. It had been Annah's idea, not his, but he'd been happy to indulge her. His reward had been a radiant smile and a kiss behind the closed door of his study that promised even greater rewards tonight.

She considered him for a long moment. 'Why are you so angry at her?'

The question caught Luca off guard and his stomach clenched. 'What makes you think I'm angry at her?

Annah hesitated. 'She told me. But even if she hadn't,' she added quickly, 'I've seen how you are with her.'

Luca felt his good mood begin to evaporate. 'And how's that?'

'Stilted,' she said. 'The tension between you is obvious, Luca.'

He shook his head. 'It's in the past. It's not important.'

She sent him an incredulous look. 'How can you say that when it still affects your relationship with her?'

He clenched his jaw.

When he didn't speak, Annah curled gentle fingers around his left biceps. 'I've told you things that weren't easy to talk about.'

He glanced down at her hand and resisted the urge to cover it with his. 'And I've talked about my father.'

And didn't it feel good? Wasn't it a relief, after five years of isolation and loneliness, to finally feel able to talk to someone?

Ruthlessly, he ignored the voice in his head. 'Why does it matter?'

'Because you're Ethan's father. And Eva is his grandmother. In time, he'll come to love you both. If there's tension between you, it will affect him.'

Luca rubbed his hand over his chin. His mother had spoken of their relationship to Annah? He supposed it was inevitable. The women got along. He was happy they did. It didn't hurt for Annah to have some female company.

But to make her understand his side of things, he'd have to tell her something ugly.

'Luca?' she pressed when he was silent too long.

He hefted out a breath. Fixed his gaze on a distant point across the valley. 'When I was sixteen my father took me to a meeting. It was in the evening, so I assumed it was a business dinner. My father said it would be my initiation into the business, and I felt… important, I suppose.' He shook his head. He'd been so naive. So oblivious to what awaited him. 'But we didn't go to a restaurant. We went to a warehouse. Some of my father's men were already there—with a man they'd beaten half to death.'

He heard Annah gasp, felt her fingers tighten on

his arm. Her touch comforted. Kept him anchored in the here and now even as the horror of the scene replayed in his head. 'Franco said the man had betrayed him—betrayed *us*—and we had to teach him a lesson. Send a message to others who would do the same. He put a hammer in my hand. Ordered me to break the poor bastard's fingers.'

Another gasp.

Luca dragged his hand across his mouth, swallowed the acrid taste of bile.

'You didn't do it.' Annah's voice was a fierce whisper, her words a statement, not a question.

Luca looked at her, something tight inside him unravelling at her conviction that he would never commit such an atrocity. 'No,' he said, his voice hoarse. 'I didn't. I threw the hammer down and walked out.' He'd been angry. Sick to his stomach. Disillusioned. 'The next morning I confronted my mother. Asked her if she knew who Franco was. *What* he was.' His jaw tightened. 'She said she'd known since Enzo and I were little.'

He turned his gaze to the meadow. His mother knelt on the ground behind his son, her arms around him, helping to hold the kite's spool. A memory of her doing the same thing with him flashed unbidden into his head.

'Did she say anything else?'

He made a rough sound. 'She said it was "complicated".'

'Maybe it was,' Annah said softly.

He shook his head. 'It was simple. She lied to me for sixteen years. Let me believe my father was a decent man. Let me *idolise* him.'

Annah was silent a moment. 'Perhaps she wanted to protect you.'

He met her eyes. 'It had nothing to do with me, or Enzo. She loved my father. That was her vice— her weakness.'

Annah's brows knitted. 'You think love is a weakness?'

'I think it clouds people's judgement,' he said. 'Warps their view of things.' A lesson Luca had learned the hard way and would never forget. Love affected a person's ability to make the right decisions. The tough decisions. Ones that could ultimately tip the scale between life and death. A man had to be strong to protect the people he cared about. Not weak.

Annah's hand withdrew from his arm, but he captured her fingers, drew her close to him and stole a brief kiss. 'Let's not talk of such things.' He stroked the underside of her wrist and felt her pulse flutter. 'It's a beautiful day. And I have a surprise back at the villa.'

She drew back, gave him an arch look. 'Isn't it a little early for bed?'

Luca laughed, a deep chuckle of amusement that expanded his chest, and marvelled at her ability to lift his mood.

* * *

'You bought him a puppy?'

Annah couldn't keep the dismay from her voice. But she wasn't sure Luca noticed or even heard her speak over Ethan's squeals of delight.

He dropped to his knees on the flagstone terrace, and the little chocolate Labrador pup planted his floppy paws on Ethan's chest and licked his face. It was the most adorable thing to watch—and it made Annah as mad as hell.

For Ethan's sake, however, she pasted on a happy expression and kept it up for almost an hour as they took afternoon tea on the terrace. Just when she feared her face would crack from the effort of smiling, Eva, who no doubt detected the tension, suggested to Ethan they go and sort out some sleeping quarters for the puppy.

Annah sent the older woman a grateful look and waited till she and Ethan were out of earshot before speaking. 'Why did you do that?'

Luca's expression was perplexed. 'The dog is a gift,' he said evenly. 'And if I am not mistaken, our son is delighted by it.'

'Why didn't you ask me first?'

Luca frowned. His tone changed. 'Do I require your permission to give my own child a gift?'

'Yes!' She pushed off her chair and stalked down the steps into the gardens. After a moment, heavy footsteps crunched on the gravel path behind her.

'Cara.'

She ignored him, even though she knew she was being mulish. She veered onto the path that led through a grove of tall trees to the pond.

'Annah!'

She couldn't out-stride him. His legs were too powerful and long. He caught her wrist, spun her round, and pulled her tightly against him.

Something hotter and even more turbulent than anger charged the air.

His head lowered and Annah hated herself for closing her eyes and raising her mouth to receive his kiss. For craving his touch even when she was mad at him. Maybe she was overreacting to the puppy. She'd felt off-kilter ever since Luca had told her that shocking story.

Suddenly, he cursed and straightened. He eased her away from him, and she opened her eyes, torn between disappointment and relief.

He stared down at her for a moment, tight-jawed, then took her hand and led her in a different direction through the trees. They emerged at the swimming pool, near the hot tub where they'd fooled around late last night after everyone else had retired. By the time he sat her down in a chair beside the pool, she wasn't sure whether the brisk walk or a sudden case of nerves had rendered her breathless.

Luca pulled his chair round so he faced her. 'Tell me what I have done wrong, *cara*.'

She took a deep breath to calm herself. 'Ethan

will miss that puppy when we go home,' she said after a moment.

'Is that a bad thing? He will look forward to returning.'

'Exactly.' Luca frowned, and she bit her lip. 'I'm sorry,' she said. 'I don't mean it like that. I know Sicily will become Ethan's home as much as England. It's just…' She looked down at her hands.

'Just what?' he prompted.

She gave a helpless shrug. 'It's not just the puppy. I can't compete with all of this, Luca.' She swept her hand at their surroundings. 'It's amazing. Sooner or later, Ethan will realise it, too. What if he chooses this over England? What if—?' Her throat closed. Swallowing, she forced herself to voice her greatest fear. 'What if he chooses you over me?'

Luca reached for her hand, lifted it to his mouth, and kissed her fingers in that very Italian way of his. 'This is not a competition, *cara*. We both want what is best for our son, yes?'

'Of course.'

He leaned forward, forearms on his thighs, her hand clasped between both of his. 'What if Ethan did not have to choose between England and Sicily?'

She frowned. 'What do you mean?'

'What if he had just one home—a stable home with both parents?'

'You mean…here?'

'Yes.'

Her heart rate sped up. 'You're suggesting Ethan and I live here…permanently?'

'As a family.'

She stared. 'You and I…'

'Would marry.'

Shock jolted through Annah's body. Her mouth went dry, her jaw slack.

Was he serious?

'Yes,' he said, making her realise she'd voiced the question aloud.

'Luca…' She fell silent, her brain grappling with the enormity of what he suggested. 'I… I don't know what to say…'

'Say you will think about it.'

His thumb stroked circles across her palm, sending hot streaks of sensation through her. Making it hard to concentrate. 'It… It seems so drastic.'

Luca's eyebrows drew down. 'Giving our son a stable home and family life is drastic?' His dark eyes sharpened on hers. 'Do you like the idea of shipping him back and forth between two countries?'

'No, but—'

'Then why would you not at least consider an alternative?'

She took an unsteady breath. 'You're talking about a marriage of convenience, Luca.'

'Or a marriage with benefits,' he countered, 'depending on how you look at it.' One side of his mouth kicked up in a smile that drove a barb of heat straight into her feminine core.

She swallowed. Oh, how easy it was to imagine spending a lifetime in Luca's bed! But great sex was hardly a strong foundation for marriage. What about when they hit a rough patch? Or grew tired of each other? Would Luca look elsewhere for pleasure?

The thought made her chest tighten painfully.

And what of love?

Luca had a clear opinion on the subject, but Annah's thoughts were muddled. Her mother's endless, desperate quest for romantic love had only ever left Rachel miserable and unfulfilled, so wasn't it better not to look for love in the first place?

Or did she *want* Luca to love her?

Annah pushed the thought away and rubbed her forehead. 'I wouldn't just be leaving England,' she said, focusing on practicalities. 'I'd be leaving Chloe and our business. My work. What would I do here, Luca? Swan around being pampered and waited on?' She shook her head. 'It's not my style.'

Luca's expression was undaunted. 'When we expand the winery, I'll need an events manager,' he said. 'I think you'd be amazing at something like that.'

She glanced at him. 'Really?'

'Yes.'

Her heart gave a little kick. She wasn't naive—she understood he was sweetening the pot—but she got the feeling his faith in her ability was genuine.

But if she said yes, it wasn't the only role she'd fulfil. She would become Luca's wife.

His wife.

The idea made her feel as giddy and breathless as she had in the helicopter the other day when they'd flown over the gaping craters of Mount Etna.

She snatched a breath. 'This is…a lot to take in. I need time to think.'

'Of course,' he said smoothly. 'Why don't you extend your stay for another week, or a few days at least? Use the time to think. Talk with me about your concerns.'

She hesitated, her pulse leaping at the prospect of more time with Luca. 'I'd have to call Chloe,' she said carefully. 'See if she can do without me for a bit longer.'

With any luck, her friend would talk some sense into her.

Luca took Annah's hand and helped her from the back of the SUV.

When she stood next to him on the cobbled sidewalk, he murmured in her ear, 'You look stunning tonight, *dolcezza*.'

A pretty pink blush stained her cheeks. 'Thank you.' She glanced down at her dress. 'Your mother spotted this and encouraged me to try it on when we were shopping yesterday.'

Luca's eyebrows rose. His mother had helped Annah choose this sexy, shimmery midnight-blue dress? He ran his gaze over the fitted bodice and short, flared skirt that swished tantalisingly around her long legs.

Points to Eva, he conceded—on top of points for looking after Ethan this evening.

He pressed his hand to Annah's back and guided her through the entrance to the small, elegant restaurant tucked down a quiet side street in the heart of the old city.

Almost a week had passed since he'd put his proposal to her by the pool. He'd resisted pressing for an answer. Her request for time to consider his proposal wasn't unreasonable. Yet with each day, each *hour* that went by without her announcing her decision, his patience dwindled.

He wanted Annah.

That realisation had crystallised in his mind this last week.

Not just because she was his child's mother and legally binding her to him guaranteed Luca a permanent role in their son's life.

He wanted *her*. As his lover. His partner.

He was thirty years old. Even had he not discovered he had a son, he would have contemplated marriage and children within the next few years.

Why look elsewhere for a suitable wife when the perfect woman was under his nose?

In the restaurant, a waiter seated them at an intimate, candlelit table, filled their water glasses, and smiled approvingly when Luca ordered an expensive bottle of wine.

Once they were alone, he settled his gaze on Annah and felt the slow glide of heat through his body. She was exquisite. He couldn't imagine a time when he would stop desiring her. He dropped his gaze to her shapely lips and recalled how she'd knelt before him last night and boldly taken him in her mouth.

Her cheeks coloured. She knew what he was thinking. 'Luca,' she whispered, a hint of admonishment in her tone. 'Stop.'

He let a slow smile curve his mouth. 'I missed you, *cara*.'

Her laugh was breathy. 'You saw me just this morning.'

He turned his smile into a semi-serious scowl. He'd seen a flash of delectable derriere in the grey predawn light as she'd thrown on her clothes and scurried from his room some time before six a.m. Without thinking, he said, 'I look forward to the day we don't have to sneak about like teenagers.'

Too late, he realised his mistake. She drew back, and the muscles at his nape tightened. Reaching across the table, he clasped her hand before she could pull it into her lap.

She frowned. 'You're assuming—'

'I'm *hoping*,' he said. 'As I have done every day for the last week. I am trying to be patient—' frustration crept into his voice despite his best efforts to keep it at bay '—but you must know only one answer will make me happy.'

Her delicate throat worked as she swallowed. 'It's a big decision…'

'Of course.' He kept his tone reasonable, even as he wondered what the hell else he had to do to convince her. 'This week has been good, yes?'

Her expression softened. 'It's been wonderful.'

His tension eased a little. They agreed on this, at least. His frustration with her indecision aside, these last seven days had been everything he had anticipated and more. When Annah insisted he not neglect his work, he recognised her desire for space and gave it to her. Each day—except for today when non-stop conference calls had occupied him—he joined Annah and Ethan for mealtimes, including breakfast.

Luca looked forward to every one of those mealtimes, many of which, at Annah's gentle urging, included his mother. Invariably, there was chatter and laughter. Ethan always greeted him with a hug that made something in his chest pull tight, and accepted, without too much pouting, that his father needed to work sometimes.

At the beginning of the week, he'd given Annah exclusive use of a four-wheel drive and knew she'd explored the far reaches of the estate. When she wanted to venture farther afield, a driver and bodyguard were at her disposal. Yesterday, for the first time, she'd entrusted Ethan's care to Luca while she and Eva went on a shopping trip. The day before, she met up with Mia and the women took Ethan and Liliana to a petting zoo.

But it was the nights that truly blew his expectations out of the water. And not only because of the mind-blowing sex. Annah was intelligent and inquisitive, genuinely interested in his work and the strides he'd made towards legitimising the family business. Their discussions invigorated him. He had never talked with a woman—never opened himself up—the way he did with Annah.

They were a good match. A *great* match. Why did she hesitate to take the next logical step?

The waiter returned with the wine. Luca banked his frustration, and they slipped into easier, safer conversation.

Throughout the meal, however, he sensed she held something back. After they'd ordered dessert, he finally said, 'What's on your mind, *dolcezza*?'

Her eyes met his. She hesitated, bit her lip. Then, 'Will you tell me what happened to your brother?'

Instantly, his stomach went hard. Once before, during the week, she had broached the subject of Enzo, but Luca had quickly deflected—as he did now. 'That's not a conversation for the dinner table.'

A determined light entered her eyes. 'Why do I get the feeling there's no right place for that conversation?'

'Because I don't want to talk about it,' he said, tension zinging into his shoulders.

'Why?'

He set his jaw. 'Why do you care?' he shot back.

She blinked, hurt flashing across her face, and he cursed inwardly.

Her voice was quiet. 'Because you're the man I'm thinking about marrying. About spending the rest of my life with. I want to understand you. I think your brother's death affected you deeply, and I think you've probably never talked about it to anyone.' She paused, her chin tilted at a slightly defiant angle, blue eyes glistening in the candlelight. 'And because I *do* care, Luca. Our lives are inextricably linked now through Ethan. Regardless of what decision I make, I will always care about you.'

Annah's heart thudded unevenly. She had just told Luca she cared about him, and the admission made her feel as stripped bare and vulnerable as if she sat in the restaurant naked.

Silence blanketed the table, Luca's expression so taut she longed to reach across, cup his face, and smooth her thumbs over his ravaged features.

She balled her hands tightly in her lap.

She could barely credit she was here and not back in England. Agreeing to extend her and Ethan's stay had surprised herself as much as it delighted Luca.

Chloe had not proven the fount of good sense Annah had hoped for.

'Oh, my God!' she'd cried, her squeal forcing Annah to pull the phone away from her ear. 'He's fallen for you!'

Annah had tried to temper her friend's excitement. 'He hasn't. This is about Ethan. Luca's proposing has nothing to do with love.' Not that it'd been a proposal in the traditional sense. Which was fine. She didn't need romance.

Or love? a little voice had whispered before Annah quickly silenced it.

'Stay,' Chloe had insisted. 'Everything's ticking along here just fine.'

And now here she sat, her pulse racing, knowing instinctively this was important. A puzzle piece she had to slot into place if she were to have any hope of truly understanding Luca.

'My brother died in prison,' he said suddenly.

Shock sent her eyes wide, but she stifled her gasp and kept silent, afraid that so much as a murmur of sympathy might stop him telling the story.

He picked up his wine, finished it in a single gulp, and put the glass down. 'Enzo was younger than me and more susceptible to our father's influence,' he said, his gaze fixating on his empty glass. 'When I came back after my first year at university in the States, he was…different. It cemented my determination to return when I completed my studies. I thought I could not only change Franco, but save Enzo from ending up like him.'

He shook his head, his mouth hard. 'But he was too entrenched. Too far gone. I couldn't get through to him. After I fell out with Franco and moved to New York, Enzo refused to accept even a phone call from me.'

He was silent a moment. Annah's throat grew painfully tight. She badly wanted to reach for his hand, offer comfort, but his gaze was turned inward, focused on the past, and she didn't want to jolt him.

'Enzo was imprisoned for arson and manslaughter. He was doing our father's dirty work and set fire to a retail shop. His defence counsel claimed he didn't know the owner was inside the premises at the time.' His gaze found hers, and the torment in his eyes broke her heart. 'I want to believe that, but I… I don't know.'

Annah couldn't hold back. She slid her hand across the white linen tablecloth and gripped Luca's. 'What happened?' she asked.

'A fight in the prison… He took a shiv in the chest, didn't survive the wound.'

It was so horrible she couldn't think of any words to say. Her heart wrenched for Eva, too. In a way, she'd lost her youngest son twice—first to corruption, then to death.

'I'm so sorry you lost him,' she whispered.

He turned his palm up, wrapped his fingers around Annah's. 'Sometimes life takes, sometimes it gives. I lost Enzo, but I found Ethan…' he looked up from their joined hands '…and you.'

Annah's heart gave a wild flutter. How was she supposed to resist this beautiful, tortured man? A desire to be skin to skin with him, to entwine her body with his and feel him moving inside her, rose with such intensity it stole her breath. She sent him a look she hoped was sultry enough to telegraph her need. 'I know we've already ordered dessert, but…'

She let the sentence hang, her breath catching when one of those slow smiles that always accelerated her heart rate touched Luca's mouth.

'I'll get the bill,' he said.

Minutes later they stood outside on the cobblestones waiting for Mario, who was both their driver and bodyguard tonight.

Luca pulled Annah's hips against him, letting her feel the hard ridge of his arousal, and kissed her intimately. 'I'm not sure I can wait,' he growled against her mouth. 'How do you feel about sex in the back of the SUV?'

A breathless laugh tumbled from Annah's throat, and when Mario pulled up seconds later she couldn't stop a hot blush from engulfing her cheeks. He leapt out to open the rear door, and she moved towards the vehicle. But the heel of her stiletto caught in the uneven cobblestones and she stepped right out of it.

'I've got it,' said Mario, dropping to his haunches to retrieve the shoe.

She turned an embarrassed smile to Luca, but found herself staring at his back. Her smile turned quizzical. 'Luca?'

He didn't turn around. 'Go inside the restaurant, Annah.'

His voice was calm, but something in his tone made the hairs at her nape stand on end. 'What's wrong?' she breathed, stepping sideways to see around Luca at the same instant Mario dropped her shoe and bolted to his feet.

Annah froze, her heart slamming violently against her ribs.

A man—a young man, possibly even a teenager—stood in the darkened cobblestone street about three metres from them. His face was flushed and screwed up in a grimace, but she couldn't tell if it was rage or fear contorting his features. His right arm was fully extended in front of him. In his hand he gripped a gun—and the gun was aimed at Luca's heart.

A terrible sound tore from Annah's throat. She lunged for Luca, not thinking. Acting on impulse. Driven by fear and a deep, powerful instinct to protect her child's father.

The boy's eyes widened and the gun swung wildly towards her.

Luca threw his body in front of hers, and then an arm clamped around her waist from behind, strong as steel, dragging her backwards. Mario.

'No!' she cried. But he was too strong. She flailed and kicked, one foot still shoeless, as he held her off the ground, turning so that his back was between her and the shooter. He bundled her into the restaurant, drawing startled looks and exclamations from patrons and waiting staff.

After an urgent exchange with the maître d', Mario turned to her, his hands, big as oven mitts, folding over her shoulders. 'Stay here. I am going through the kitchen to the alley.'

She grabbed at his arm with both hands. 'Please don't let anything happen to him, Mario. I—' She gulped in a breath, cutting off her sentence, but the words rang in her head regardless.

I love him.

Then Mario was gone.

Violent tremors ran through Annah's legs. Her knees gave out and she sagged against a wall, sliding down until her bottom hit the floor. Vaguely, she was aware of restaurant staff herding diners away from the windows. Someone grabbed hold of her trembling hand and gently squeezed, murmuring words of reassurance.

Her vision blurred and she closed her eyes. Around her, everything seemed to slow, the noise growing muffled, until all she heard was the loud thud of her heartbeat pulsing in time with her thoughts.

Please, please, please don't let him get hurt. Please, please, please—

'Annah.'

Her eyes flew open. Frantically she blinked, trying to focus on the figure kneeling in front of her. A sob choked from her throat. 'Luca!' She threw her arms around him. 'Oh, my God!'

He gathered her up, walked to a chair and sat, settling her on his lap.

She drew back, her gaze darting across his shirt front, looking for injuries. Blood. 'Are you okay? Are you hurt? What happened?'

'I'm fine,' he said, but his voice was hoarse.

'Mario?'

'He's okay. He disarmed the boy.'

'Who was he?'

Luca shook his head. 'Not now, *cara*. I'll tell you everything later. The police are here. I need to deal with them, make a statement. Someone is going to take you home.'

Annah frowned. 'No. I'm staying with you.'

But he gently removed her arms from around his neck and stood.

She protested all the way to the car. Luca ignored her entreaties, put her in the back seat, and leaned in to kiss her. Their lips clung for a long moment, then he pulled back.

'I'll see you soon,' he said. And he closed the door.

CHAPTER TEN

ANNAH CREPT INTO Ethan's room. Careful not to wake him, she lay on the big bed and curled up on her side so she could watch him sleep. She didn't care if she creased her dress; she'd get changed in a few minutes. She just wanted to lie here first, take comfort from being near her little boy.

She'd arrived back at the villa ten minutes ago. Luca had called his mother, and Eva had been waiting, a worried look pleating her brow. They'd hugged, and Annah had assured Eva she was okay before heading upstairs.

She took a deep breath and slowly released it, but her heart still beat a crazy tattoo in her chest. *Adrenaline*. That was all it was. Wasn't it normal to feel jittery after a scare?

But deep down she knew it was more than that.

I love him.

She squeezed her eyes shut as if she could will away the knowledge.

On her way back to the villa, alone in the back

of the SUV, she'd tried telling herself she was mistaken. That her heightened emotions in the midst of the drama had made her mistake fear and concern for love.

But she was lying to herself, afraid to acknowledge the truth. She had fallen in love with Luca—in a little over half a month.

Was that possible? To fall in love so quickly?

Yet hadn't she fallen in love, just a tiny bit, on that night in London five years ago? Hadn't a part of her clung to the memory of him as a tender, passionate lover even after she'd convinced herself he'd cruelly abandoned her?

She shivered, the weight of a grim realisation pressing on her chest.

Luca didn't believe in love.

Which meant Annah had made the one mistake of her mother's she'd sworn she would never make.

She'd fallen in love with a man who would never love her back.

'Mummy!'

Annah jolted awake.

'You slept in your dress!'

'What?' She blinked and sat up so fast her head spun. A giggle drew her attention to Ethan, who knelt beside her on the bed. She glanced around, saw the sunlight poking through the gaps in the curtains.

It was morning?

She looked down at her crumpled dress. In an

instant, everything rushed back: the restaurant; the young man with the gun; her unsettling revelation.

A soft throw was draped over her legs. Someone must have put it over her during the night. Luca?

An urgent desire to see him—to check with her own eyes that he was okay—gripped her chest.

She looked at Ethan, put her arms around him, and hugged him tight. 'Morning, kiddo. How 'bout we get dressed and go have some breakfast?'

'Yes!'

A short while later, they made their way downstairs to the sunlit breakfast room where their days had routinely commenced over the last couple of weeks. Luca was already seated at the table, and Annah's heart leapt at the sight of him. Clean-shaven and wearing an open-necked white shirt with rolled-up sleeves, he looked as handsome and vital as ever.

Annah wanted to launch into his arms, but Ethan beat her to it.

Luca's eyes met hers above Ethan's head, dark and questioning, and she sent him a sturdy smile: *I'm fine.*

He set Ethan down, then dropped a chaste kiss on her cheek and murmured, 'We need to talk.'

'We do,' Annah agreed. She sat at the table and poured herself a coffee. She couldn't manage food. Her stomach quivered too much with nerves. But she was aware of something else, too. A small flicker of hope she knew she should extinguish yet couldn't.

Eva turned up soon afterwards, and when she

suggested to Ethan they walk the puppy—who he'd named Timmy—after breakfast, Annah wanted to hug the older woman.

Once alone, Luca and Annah went straight to his study. The instant the door closed, his arms came around her and pulled her close. Annah couldn't help herself. She sagged against him, pressed her face against his shirt, and breathed in his scent.

Tipping her chin up, he set his mouth against hers in a slow, lingering kiss that warmed her body from the inside out.

Finally, they eased apart.

'You were asleep when I got back,' he said. 'I didn't want to disturb you.'

'Did you put the blanket over me?'

'Yes.'

'I wish you'd woken me.'

His smile was rueful. 'I was tempted.' He smoothed her hair back, his face etched with concern. 'Are you okay?'

'Yes,' she said. 'Will you tell me what that was all about last night?'

He blew out his breath. 'A messed-up kid with an axe to grind.' Clasping her hand, he led her to a brown leather sofa and tugged her down beside him. 'His father's an ex-employee. The man was fencing stolen goods through one of the warehouses. I fired him last week and had criminal charges brought against him.'

It took her a moment to digest that. 'But why come

after you? You did what any employer would do. You could hardly let him get away with it!'

Luca's expression was grim. 'The boy thinks I should have punished his father the old way.'

'The old way?'

'My father's way.'

Understanding dawned, sending a cold shiver up Annah's spine. 'How could that possibly be better?'

'A man heals from a beating, even a kneecapping, and still has his freedom. But prison...' Luca shook his head. 'According to the boy, I've not only stolen his father's freedom, I've deprived his family of their main breadwinner.'

'That's warped thinking.'

'I agree. But others don't. I fired the company's security chief three weeks ago because he sanctioned the beating of a young man caught stealing.' He rubbed his thumb and forefinger over his eyelids, and for all the strength and vitality he radiated, Luca suddenly looked tired.

Emotion bloomed in Annah's chest. She placed her palm against his jaw. 'You're a good man, Luca, and I'm proud that you're Ethan's father,' she said, holding his gaze so he'd see she meant it.

He wrapped his fingers around her wrist, kissed the base of her thumb. 'Proud enough to marry me, *cara*?'

Annah's heart rate sped up. Heat scored her cheeks at the very thought of the question hovering on her tongue. But she had to ask. Had to know the answer. She drew a deep breath. 'Do you think you could one day grow to love me?'

For the span of several heartbeats, Luca was utterly still. Even his expression was frozen. Then his eyebrows plunged. His hand dropped from her wrist. 'You know my feelings on that subject.'

Awkwardly, Annah lowered her hand from his jaw. 'Yes, but...' Her voice faltered. This was every bit as difficult as she'd imagined. But she couldn't run from this conversation. Not when the outcome would affect her future and, more importantly, Ethan's. 'What if you're wrong? What if love isn't a weakness? What if...?' She cast around for the right words. 'What if love is the only thing strong enough to hold a family together? To hold a marriage together?'

He drew back, looking at her as if she'd spouted something outrageous. 'Why are you raising this at the eleventh hour when you know where I stand on it?'

Because last night changed everything. Last night I realised I love you.

'Because it's important,' she said.

'Why?'

She hesitated. 'Because I'm not sure I can settle for a loveless marriage.' She held her breath, watched his jaw muscles clench and release.

'What about everything else that can make a partnership strong?' he challenged. 'Loyalty. Commitment. Respect. Friendship.'

'Those are wonderful things—'

He cut her off. 'Then why aren't they enough?'

She looked away, the glow of hope in her heart fading like a dying ember.

After a moment, Luca leaned in, took her hand in his. His voice softened. '*Cara*, I know last night was frightening. But I will never let anything happen to you or Ethan. If you are worried, I can increase security, assign you extra—'

She shook her head. 'It's not about that, Luca. You would protect us with your life—so would Mario. Or any of your men. I know that.' It wasn't Luca's world she feared. Last night's run-in with the troubled teen was, by the sound of things, an isolated incident. Most days, the risk of falling victim to someone with a vendetta against Luca was probably no greater than the risk of being run over on a pedestrian crossing by a distracted driver in London. No. The thing she feared most right now was Luca crushing her foolish, vulnerable heart. She swallowed. 'How do you know love will make you weak when you won't even let yourself try?'

'Because I *do* know,' he said, his voice low and hard. Releasing her hand, he stood suddenly and stalked to the window. Hands thrust in his pockets, he stared out.

Forcing her legs to move, dismayed to find they trembled, she got up and followed. Stopping beside him, she set her hand on his shoulder, felt the tension vibrating in his muscles. 'How?' she pressed. 'Tell me, Luca. Help me understand.'

There was a long silence before he spoke. When he did, he didn't look at her. 'Not long before that final falling-out with Franco, a prosecutor secretly approached me. I don't know how, but he knew my father and I had conflicting values. Different visions for the family business. He wanted me to gather evidence from inside Franco's illegal operations. The kind of evidence that could have put him away for a long time.' He paused, his jaw tight. 'I should have done it, but I didn't. Somewhere inside me there was still that kid who'd idolised his father. Who'd loved his father.' He practically spat the word *loved*. 'Even after that final confrontation with Franco, I couldn't betray him—not to that extent. So I chose exile instead. Walked away from the business, the family, and went to New York.'

He turned to face her, the movement so abrupt it dislodged her hand from his shoulder. 'Love made me soft. Incapable of doing what needed to be done. If I had, Franco would have gone to prison. His hold over Enzo would have ended. My brother would still be alive.'

The torment in Luca's eyes broke Annah's heart. What was it he'd said about her mother when Annah had wondered aloud why Rachel hadn't given her up for adoption? *Perhaps she loved you too much to do the right thing.* At the time she hadn't understood the strange remark. Now it made sense. She looked into his eyes. 'You don't know that, Luca.'

'I do know it.' Lifting his hands, he stroked over her shoulders, down her upper arms. He breathed in deeply, exhaled slowly. 'I'm sorry, Annah. I can't be weak like that again. I can't love and protect at the same time.'

Frustration made the backs of her eyes burn. 'Oh, Luca.' Her voice choked. 'Don't you see? It's your emotion and your compassion for people that make you strong.'

He shook his head, not willing to entertain any other perspective.

A sudden, heart-rending sense of loss and finality swept over her.

Luca was capable of love. She didn't doubt it for a moment. But he would never surrender to it. Never make himself vulnerable. He offered her so much—security, commitment, family, their amazing physical connection. But if he didn't let himself love, he would always hold a part of himself back from her—and from Ethan.

Sadness overwhelmed her.

For the first time in Annah's life she experienced a pang of sympathy for her mother—because now she knew how it felt to desperately want a man's love.

He was losing her.

Luca could see it in the way her eyes cooled and her expression shuttered.

A cold fist clamped his chest. In his brain, a denial roared. This was *not* happening. He would not allow it.

Last night, in that split second when she'd drawn the kid's attention and the gun had swung towards her, he'd realised two things. First, he could not countenance even the idea of losing Annah. Second, it was he who had placed her in harm's way. He shouldn't have taken her out of the restaurant before Mario arrived. He sure as hell shouldn't have stood on the street kissing her like some besotted fool, oblivious to potential dangers.

It reinforced what he already knew—what he had just tried to explain to her.

He couldn't protect and love at the same time.

'Annah—'

'Don't.' She shook her head, her eyes sliding away from his. 'There's no point. We're never going to agree. We want different things.'

He set his jaw, everything in him rebelling against that statement. 'We both want what's best for Ethan.'

She pulled away from his hold. Reluctantly, he let go.

'Of course,' she said. 'But that doesn't mean we'll agree on what is best.'

His brows drew down. 'You don't think our son deserves a stable home and family life with both his parents?'

Her eyes met his. 'I think he deserves a better

example of marriage than two parents who'll never love each other.'

Frustration simmered in his blood. 'So this is your final answer?' His voice was laced with disbelief. 'You're rejecting my proposal?'

For a moment, her mouth trembled. Then she firmed her chin. 'Yes.'

Anger and desperation—and something akin to hurt—sank sharp claws in his gut. 'I won't be a part-time father, Annah. It's unacceptable.'

Her eyebrows snapped together. 'What are you saying?'

The words bolted from his throat before he could stop them. 'I'm saying don't force my hand.'

'Force…?' Her eyes widened. Comprehending. 'You would sue for sole custody?' Her voice was a horrified whisper. And then her expression changed. In an instant, her eyes were no longer the crystal blue of a summer sky but a dark, stormy indigo. 'I'll fight you,' she said in a low voice. 'I don't care how much it costs or how good your lawyers are. I'm Ethan's *mother*. You can't take him from me.'

Instantly, a tsunami of regret and self-disgust barrelled through him. *Dammit.* Why could he not harness his emotions around her?

'Annah…' He reached for her, but she stepped back. He dropped his arms to his sides. 'Forgive me,' he said, his throat stiff with remorse. 'That was my temper speaking. I would never separate you from our son.'

She looked at him for a long time before speaking. 'I think Ethan and I should leave this afternoon.'

His gut tightened. 'You're not scheduled to go until tomorrow.'

'I don't see the point in staying another night.'

He fought the urge to pull her into his arms and remind her of their powerful chemistry. Of what she would deny herself. Deny *him*.

'Fine,' he said. 'I'll make the necessary arrangements.'

His voice carried a hollow ring, but it was nothing compared to the sudden, yawning chasm inside him.

CHAPTER ELEVEN

'MAY I JOIN YOU?'

Luca turned his head at the sound of his mother's voice. He hesitated to respond. He had no particular desire for company, but neither did he have an excuse to be uncivil. After a moment, he gestured with his whisky glass to an adjacent chair on the terrace.

Eva sat, a snifter of brandy cradled in her hand, and for several minutes they sipped their drinks in silence.

Eventually, she spoke. 'I miss them.'

Luca took a swig of whisky. *So do I.* Every day for three weeks, he'd missed them. How the hell he was meant to feel satisfied with twice-weekly video calls with Ethan and the stilted two-second greetings he got each time from Annah, he had no idea.

It wouldn't do for the long term, but right now he was giving her the space she'd requested.

He stared into his glass, swirling the whisky, disgruntled at its inability to expunge the cold, hollow sensation from his stomach.

'I tried to leave him once.'

Luca's hand stilled. He raised his head and looked at his mother. She sipped her brandy, staring out over the moonlit gardens, her gaze fixed on some point in the distance.

'I'd learned he'd taken a mistress,' she said quietly, 'but that wasn't the only reason. Other things had begun to disturb me. There was a…darkness in Franco I hadn't seen in him when we married. It frightened me, so I took you boys to Naples.' She glanced at him. 'You were only eight, so you may not remember.'

Luca frowned, scouring his memory. 'I remember,' he said slowly. His mother had said they were going on holiday, and Luca had thought it strange because they never took holidays without his father.

'I thought my parents would help me,' she said. 'But your grandfather was too traditional. He told me a woman had no right to break her marriage vows, no matter what. He called Franco and… Well, that was that.'

Luca dug deeper into his memory. Yes. He remembered his father arriving in Naples. Remembered being happy to see him. But not much else. He was an eight-year-old boy, busy playing outdoors with his brother or sneaking into his grandmother's kitchen to gorge on her baking. They stayed a few more days with his grandparents, then travelled back to Sicily as a family.

How furious must Franco have been with his mother?

Luca's gut rolled uneasily. 'Were there…repercussions?'

'Not physical ones. It might be hard to believe, but Franco never laid a hand on me in anger. But he was furious like I'd never seen before.' She paused, eyes lowering to her glass. 'After a week of me barely speaking to him, he had all of my personal possessions packed into suitcases and put in the foyer. Then he laid out my choices. Stay and be an obedient wife, or leave—and never see my boys again.' Eva's chin lifted. She looked at Luca. 'I hauled those cases up the stairs one by one and unpacked them, because for me there was no choice—I couldn't leave you and Enzo.'

Luca felt his throat thicken. He didn't know what to say. He looked away, but Eva leaned forward and touched his arm.

'I know you think I was weak for loving your father,' she said. 'But the truth is I stopped loving him a long time ago. It was my love for you and Enzo that made me *strong*. Strong enough to endure an unhappy marriage. Strong enough to stay so I could try to protect you.'

Luca swallowed. In the back of his mind, words Annah had spoken three weeks ago bounced and echoed. *'It's your emotion and your compassion for people that make you strong.'*

He looked into Eva's face. 'Why did you let me believe in him for so long?'

Her sigh was heavy. 'I couldn't risk turning you against him when you were young—Franco would have known. I hoped the right time would present itself as you got older, but...' She grimaced. 'I waited too long.'

'And then we both failed Enzo,' he said darkly.

Eva shook her head, sorrow etched on her features. 'Enzo wasn't strong like you. He was impressionable. Always wanting to please his *papà*. I saw that same darkness in him that I saw in Franco. Nothing would have changed your brother—not even Franco going to prison.'

Luca looked at her sharply.

'Yes, son,' she said. 'I know more than you think—including the fact that you love Annah.'

Luca's head jerked back. He opened his mouth to disabuse her of that notion, but she didn't let him get a word in.

'Do you think I didn't see how you looked at her over the breakfast table every morning?' She shook her head, though a smile touched her lips. 'I also know you threw yourself between her and the gunman outside the restaurant that night.'

A scowl formed on his face. 'Who told you that?'

'I have my sources.' Eva's smile was only slightly smug. 'That sounds to me like the action of a man protecting the woman he loves.' She paused. 'I also heard Annah did something similar—trying to protect you.'

Eva stood up, looked down at him for a long moment. 'You might want to think about why she did that,' she said.

And then she turned and went back inside, leaving Luca alone with his thoughts.

Annah's hands shook so badly she could barely hold the mug of tea Chloe handed her without spilling it.

She took a sip, but her writhing stomach didn't appreciate even that tiny bit of liquid. She put the mug down, turned imploring eyes to Chloe's boyfriend, Ben, who looked suitably serious and official in his police uniform. 'Please,' she said, her throat hoarse after forty-five minutes walking the rapidly darkening woods, shouting Ethan's name. 'I just want to be out there looking, not sitting here answering a million questions.'

Chloe's arms came around her, and for a second, as much as she appreciated her friend, Annah wished it was Luca's arms offering her strength and support.

Then it occurred to her that he was more likely to throttle her than offer comfort when he found out their son was missing and it was *her* fault.

She pressed her lips together, holding back tears.

'We're getting a co-ordinated search underway,' Ben said, his tone professional but sympathetic. 'Plenty of volunteers have turned up, so, Annah, you should stay here.'

'What?' She gaped at Ben. 'No! I need to be out there looking for my son!'

Ben and Chloe exchanged a look.

'When we find him,' Ben said, 'the first person he'll want to see is his mother. You should be here for when that happens.'

Annah was grateful for Ben's use of *when*, not *if*, but she still wasn't happy.

Chloe squeezed Annah's shoulder. 'You're exhausted. Why don't we both stay here? We can keep the tea and coffee flowing for the volunteers.'

She *was* exhausted. It was the whole reason this had happened. She'd been sleeping terribly. Missing Luca. Second-guessing her decision to reject his proposal every time a pouting Ethan asked when they were going to see Papà and Nonna and Timmy again. She'd thrown herself into work and parenting, proving she was strong and capable—that she and Ethan didn't need anyone else.

'If only I'd got that blasted lock fixed instead of waiting for the landlord to do it,' she muttered. And if only Mister Pickles hadn't gone walkabout. She'd promised Ethan they'd look for him tomorrow, hoping the ginger tabby would turn up in the meantime. Then she'd nodded off on the sofa. When she'd woken, the kitchen door was ajar, Ethan gone.

She rubbed her temples with her fingertips, fighting to keep the panic at bay. 'Okay,' she relented. 'I'll stay.'

Then she took a deep breath, went in search of her phone, and made the call she dreaded making.

An hour later, Annah felt ready to crawl out of her skin. Pacing the floor of her flat while others were out there combing the fields and woods was driving her crazy.

'I've put some pork pies in the kitchen, dear,' said Dot from behind her. 'Can I make you a cup of tea?'

'No, thank you,' Annah said, continuing to stare out the window. The light had faded and the woods behind the flat were dark. Every now and again, a beam of light from a searcher's torch cut through the trees.

Turning away from the living-room window, she glanced down at her phone clutched in her hand. It'd been horribly silent. Had Luca picked up her message?

She paced again. He was going to be furious. She'd lost their son! Their beautiful, precious boy.

'Annah?'

Chloe's voice tugged her from her miserable thoughts. She looked to where Chloe stood in the kitchen, having paused in the act of drying a cup, her gaze directed out the window.

Chloe gave a little gasp. 'Is that...?'

Annah's skin prickled even before she turned to the window and saw Luca bounding up the steps two at a time. She blinked, barely able to believe her eyes.

How on earth...?

He burst through the door, and Dot and Chloe both gaped, wide-eyed, as he slammed to a halt and looked around. The instant his eyes found her, he stalked over, stopping close enough for her to feel the heat radiating off him.

Annah stared, confused. 'You got my message?' she croaked.

'Yes.' Under a day's worth of dark stubble, his jaw muscles worked. 'I was already in England—on my way here. My phone was off. I only listened to your message ten minutes ago.'

On his way here?

But he gave her no time to puzzle over that. 'He's still missing?' he said, his tone sharp with urgency and concern.

'Yes.' Fear and misery welled, and she blinked rapidly, afraid she'd succumb to tears and he'd see how weak and needy she felt just then. 'I'm so sorry,' she said, straightening her shoulders, bracing for his anger. 'It's all my fault.'

A rough sound came from Luca's throat, and then his arms suddenly wrapped around her. For a second she stiffened in surprise, but then she fell against him, choking back a sob, burying her face against his wonderfully broad chest.

This doesn't change anything, a small voice cautioned. But he felt so good—warm and strong and solid—she didn't care about anything in that moment except the fact that he was here.

He drew back, set his hands on either side of her face. 'We will find him,' he said. 'Together, yes?'

Annah nodded, her throat too tight to speak.

Then she pulled herself together and introduced him to Chloe, Dot, and George—Ben's colleague, who stood in the dining room updating grid search areas on the map spread across the table.

'This is Ethan's father,' she said, and Dot's eyes nearly popped out of her head.

George shook Luca's hand, then offered a quick overview of the searchers' progress. He glanced at Annah. 'We thought it best that Annah stay back so she's here when he's found.'

Luca's eyes narrowed on her face, and she stiffened, waiting for him to agree with everyone else. To tell her she should sit here twiddling her thumbs, going slowly insane.

'Is that what you want?' he asked.

She blinked in surprise. 'I'd rather be out there looking.'

He nodded once, then glanced around until he located Chloe, who looked slightly startled to find herself pinned by his intense gaze. 'My son knows you well, yes?'

Chloe nodded.

'Then you will stay so that if Annah's not here when he's brought back, you can reassure him,' he said, assuming command of the situation with such ease, nobody, not even George, questioned his authority. 'Annah and I will join the search.'

In less than a minute, Annah donned her jacket and walking boots, slid her phone in her pocket, and grabbed two torches.

At the bottom of the steps, something made her reach out and grab Luca's arm. He stopped and stared down at her, his eyes glittering with an intensity that sent a flood of warmth through her veins. She opened her mouth, compelled to say something, but the wild tangle of her feelings defied words.

He set his hand against the side of her face. 'We'll talk afterwards,' he said softly, his thumb caressing her cheek. 'First, we find our son.'

Thirty minutes later Luca had just bellowed Ethan's name for the hundredth time when he heard an electronic chirping sound.

He swung his torchlight in Annah's direction and saw her scrambling to pull her phone from her pocket and press it to her ear.

He sucked in a breath, his throat so raw it was painful to inhale.

This was not how he'd envisaged spending this evening when he'd departed from Sicily earlier today. For once he'd left Mario behind in Palermo and picked up a rented SUV from the private airstrip. When he'd finally remembered to check his phone and then pulled over to listen to Annah's message, he was almost here.

Mud and grass squelched under his boots as he moved closer, scrutinising her features in the pale moonlight, trying to gauge her expression. When her hand flew to her mouth, stifling a sound that was half gasp, half sob, his heart jack-knifed in his chest.

She lowered the phone, and for a second he couldn't breathe. Then she flung her arms around his neck. 'They found him, Luca,' she whispered. 'He's okay.'

Relief hit so hard, his legs quivered as if he'd just crossed the finish line of a marathon. He held Annah tightly against him. 'Where?'

'In a barn. On the other side of the woods. Someone's taking him home now.'

She pulled back and looked at him, her eyes glistening with joy and relief, and for a crazy moment Luca wanted to pull the diamond-encrusted ring from his pocket, drop to his knees in the mud, and declare his love right there and then.

But he summoned restraint. A muddy field was no place for a proper marriage proposal. And more than anything else right then, they both needed to see their son.

Back at the flat, relief shook Luca to his core all over again when he set eyes on Ethan. Although cold and tearful, he appeared unhurt, but Luca insisted on a house call from the local doctor to check him over nonetheless.

After an interminable hour Ethan was safely tucked up in bed and the police, the volunteers, the doctor, and Annah's friends were gone.

Finally, Luca had her to himself.

Except now that they were alone and the rush of adrenaline from finding Ethan had abated, those big blue eyes of hers regarded him warily.

'Why are you here, Luca?'

They stood in the kitchen, facing each other across

its width, the space so small a single stride would bridge the gap and set his body flush against hers.

For a moment longer, he resisted moving. 'Because we need to talk.'

'We could have talked on the phone.'

'Not for this,' he said. 'What I need to say has to be said in person.'

Annah's palms were damp and her heart was beating too fast as she stared at Luca. 'Why?' she asked.

He pushed away from the bench behind him. When he stepped towards her, her pulse leapt and her brain urged her to move, to put distance between them, but her legs didn't get the message.

'Because I need you to believe me when I tell you this.'

'Tell me what?' she said unsteadily, barely able to breathe for the wild flurry of emotions in her chest.

He held her gaze as he brought his hands up and framed her face.

Annah sucked in her breath, some deep intuition telling her what he was going to say. Panic and hope flared in equal measures. His lips parted, but she jerked her hand up and pressed her fingers against them. 'Don't you dare say those words unless you mean them, Luca Cavallari.' It was meant to sound like a fierce warning, but her voice was little more than a shaky whisper. 'If you're here to seduce me with lies—' She broke off, the rapidly expanding lump in her throat making it too hard to talk.

Gently, Luca pulled her arm down and then cupped her face in his hands again. She closed her eyes, afraid that her burgeoning hope would sprout wings and take flight prematurely.

'Please look at me, *cara*.'

She swallowed. He asked so nicely, how could she resist? She opened her eyes, her breath catching at the raw emotion etched on his face.

'I love you,' he said, looking into her eyes, forcing her to see the truth in his. 'I should have realised it three weeks ago, but I was so afraid of failing to do the right thing by you and Ethan that in the end I did the worst thing possible—I let you go.'

Tears scalded Annah's eyes. Blinking them away, she brought her hands up between them and placed them against his chest, assuring herself he was real. That this wasn't just another tantalising dream she'd awaken from to find herself alone and suffering with a broken heart. 'Oh, Luca.'

Dipping his head, he pressed a tender kiss on her mouth.

She kissed him back, finally allowing her heart to soar. After a long moment, she drew back and asked, 'What made you realise?'

'Besides the hole in my chest after you and Ethan left?' A wry smile twisted his lips. 'A surprising conversation with my mother, for starters.'

She looked at him in amazement. 'You and Eva talked?'

He held her close, his hands stroking up and

down her back. 'It was a conversation we should have had years ago, but I never gave her the opportunity.' Regret roughened his voice. 'Did you know she tried to leave Franco once and take Enzo and me with her?'

Annah's eyes widened. 'No. She did say that your father never would have let her take you and Enzo away, but I didn't know she'd actually tried. That must have taken tremendous courage.'

'More courage than I've ever given her credit for,' he admitted.

'What happened?' she asked, even though she feared the answer. Had Eva's husband punished her for trying to leave?

Luca's expression turned grim for a moment. 'My father brought her back. Gave her a choice. Stay and be a dutiful wife, or leave and never see me and Enzo again.'

'It wasn't really a choice, was it?' she whispered.

He shook his head. 'She sacrificed so much—her freedom, the chance to find happiness with someone else—so that she could stay for me and Enzo.'

'Because she loved you.'

'Yes,' he said hoarsely.

'Eva's a strong woman.'

'And I'm a fool for having ever thought her weak.'

Annah put her hand to his cheek. 'You're not a fool, Luca.'

He smiled ruefully. 'Don't let me off so easily, *cara*. I *am* a fool. I believed I could choose not to love—that doing so made me stronger. Less fallible.' He brushed his thumb over her cheekbone. 'But I was wrong. I don't think we get to choose love. I think love chooses us whether we're ready for it or not.'

Tears clogged her throat. 'It broke my heart to think you might never let yourself love our son.'

'Trust me,' he said, his eyes intent on hers, 'Ethan will know every single day of his life how much his father loves him.' He lifted her into his arms then and carried her to the sofa in the living room. The instant she was settled on his lap he kissed her again and she felt the familiar, delicious heat begin to build inside her.

Wrapping her arms around his neck, she whispered against his mouth, 'I love you, too.'

He pulled back, just far enough to stare in her eyes. 'I'd started to hope these past twenty-four hours,' he said, his voice thick with emotion. 'But I wasn't certain. That last day…you didn't say anything.'

'I couldn't. You were so adamant you would never love me back.' She grimaced. 'I grew up watching my mother throw herself at men, desperate to be loved. It made me angry at her for a long time—like you were angry at Eva, I suppose. I was determined to never be weak like that.' Annah had thought a lot about her mother over the last few weeks. Little by little, her bitterness towards Rachel had ebbed. In its place had come sadness and even compassion for a woman who'd spent her life searching for love when what she probably needed most was to learn to love herself.

Luca tucked his fingers beneath her chin. 'You are not weak, *cara*. You are strong. You raised our son on your own for over four years and did an amazing job.'

She tried to smile but her lips wobbled. 'Doing it on my own hasn't felt very good these last three weeks,' she confessed. 'I missed you.'

He swept a strand of hair from her face, brushed his knuckles down her cheek. 'You don't have to do it alone any more.' Shifting suddenly, he set her down on the sofa and got up. He went to his jacket, which hung on the back of a dining room chair, and returned with his hand closed around something.

Annah's heart quickened when he dropped to one knee in front of her and opened his fingers to reveal a black velvet box and, when he lifted the lid, a stunning platinum and diamond engagement ring nestled inside.

'I love you, Annah,' he said, his gaze fixed on hers. 'I want to be your husband and I want to be a father to our son. I want to love and protect you both for the rest of my life.' He paused. 'Will you marry me?'

Fresh tears filled her eyes, but this time she didn't bother fighting them. Didn't care when they slipped down her cheeks and dripped off her chin. 'Yes,' she said, and then watched him slide the gorgeous ring onto her finger. She leaned in to kiss him.

The cat flap in the kitchen door rattled and a loud *meow* pierced the air.

She pulled back, eyes widening. 'Mister Pickles!'

Leaving a trail of muddy paw prints in his wake, the cat trotted across the room and leapt onto her lap, nudging his furry body between her and Luca. Annah laughed at the less than impressed look on Luca's face. She stroked the cat's head, relieved to see him alive and well. 'You have terrible timing, Mister Pickles. But a certain little boy is going to be very happy to see you in the morning.'

With a gentle hand, Luca scooped the ginger tabby off her lap, shooed him away, and then tugged her back into his arms. 'Where were we?'

Annah took his face between her hands, her heart swelling with love and irrepressible happiness. They still had things to discuss, details to iron out, but right now all that mattered was they were together—Luca, her, and Ethan. A family.

'I think we were about here,' she said, and pressed her mouth against his.

EPILOGUE

Fourteen years later

ETHAN CAVALLARI RAN a lazy hand over his dishevelled hair as he sauntered into the breakfast room to join the rest of his family.

'Ethan!' Letting out a high-pitched squeal, his youngest sister leapt off her chair, ran across the room and launched into his arms.

He grinned, swung seven-year-old Aria onto his hip, and planted an affectionate kiss on her cheek. 'Hey, squirt.'

She grinned back. 'Mamma said I could stay up till you got here last night, but I fell asleep.'

'I know. I went up to see you and you were snoring.'

She giggled and slapped her palm against his chest. 'Was not!'

Leo, three years Aria's senior, joined in from the breakfast table. 'You were. I heard it all the way from my room.'

'It was so loud the windows rattled,' said twelve-year-old Siena, not to be outdone by her brothers when it came to teasing their little sister.

Aria poked her tongue out at Siena and Leo, but she was laughing and so were her siblings.

From opposite ends of the table, Luca and Annah locked eyes with each other and smiled. On mornings like this, when Ethan was home from university and her family was gathered around the breakfast table, Annah felt as if her heart might burst it was so full of happiness.

'Uh-oh,' Ethan said in a loud stage whisper as he set Aria back on her chair and took the one next to her. 'Don't look now, but Mum and Papà are making eyes at each other again.'

The children giggled and snickered, except for Siena, who slanted her older brother a sly smile. 'I saw you and Lili making eyes at each other at the New Year's picnic.'

Annah watched, amused, as a bright flush crept over her son's face. He and Liliana had been friends from the day they'd sat together in the courtyard of her grandparents' restaurant with crayons and colouring books. Now they were older, it wouldn't surprise Annah if their friendship deepened into something more. Mario and Mia's daughter had blossomed into a beautiful young woman and, given his blushing reaction, Ethan wasn't unaware of the fact.

Reaching for a pitcher of orange juice, he changed the subject. 'When are Nonna and Alberto arriving?'

Luca glanced at his watch. 'Couple of hours.'

'I'll collect them from the airport if you like,' Ethan offered, always eager for an excuse to drive now that he was eighteen.

'Thanks, sweetheart.' Annah smiled. 'That would be great.'

Eva and her husband lived in Rome, but they often travelled to Sicily for holidays and special occasions. Today they were arriving to spend Easter at the Cavallari Estate.

Eva had met Alberto through a mutual friend seven years ago, and the charming widower had courted her for eighteen months and then proposed.

Annah was thrilled for her mother-in-law. Alberto was a warm, kind-hearted man who loved Eva deeply. Their wedding joined a long list of family highlights that included the births of Siena, Leo, and Aria, and of course Annah and Luca's own wedding a few months after she and Ethan had moved to Sicily.

Seeing Luca repair his relationship with Eva in those early years had inspired Annah to reconnect with her own mother. To her surprise, Rachel had tearfully embraced the opportunity to mend her relationship with her daughter. For Annah, moving forward had meant burying old hurts and finding forgiveness in her heart, but letting go of all that baggage had proven incredibly liberating.

As the children bantered with one another, Annah's gaze found Luca's again. He, too, had mastered the art of forgiveness, letting go of the ill feeling he'd harboured towards his mother and, more importantly, himself. While he would always mourn the loss of Enzo, he no longer blamed himself for his brother's death.

He held her gaze, a slightly wicked smile curving one side of his mouth, and she knew he was thinking about their lovemaking in the shower that morning. Her pulse quickened. Fourteen years married and their chemistry was still electric.

Twenty minutes later, after the children had finished their breakfast and disappeared to do their own things, Luca moved to a chair close to Annah's, reached for her hand, and tugged her into his lap.

Cupping his palm around the back of her head, he drew her lips down for a slow, lingering kiss. 'I have an idea, *dolcezza*,' he said against her mouth.

Smiling, her arms looped around his neck, she pulled back to look at him. 'What?'

'Let's leave the kids with Mamma and Alberto and disappear for the weekend.'

She laughed and shook her head.

A look of mock-affront crossed his handsome features. 'Not even tempted?'

She arched an eyebrow. 'By a dirty weekend away with my husband? I'm tempted,' she assured him. 'But it's Easter and everyone's here. You know how much I love it when the family's all together.' She poked a fingertip against his chest. 'And so do you.'

His lips quirked up. 'Have I told you recently how much I love you?'

'Mmm-hmm. Just this morning, in fact.'

He splayed his hand over her stomach, a teasing light entering his eyes. 'Perhaps we made a *bambino* this morning?'

Annah pretended to scowl. 'No more babies,' she declared. 'I'm too old—and we already have four beautiful children. Besides, I'm enjoying working again.'

Fourteen years ago Luca had placed the development of the winery restaurant and function venue in Annah's hands. He'd given support and advice when she'd sought it, but otherwise trusted her and the winery manager to run with the venture and make it a resounding success—which they had. Annah had loved every minute of it and kept her hand in right up until Aria was born, at which point, with four children to keep her on her toes, she'd decided to devote herself to full-time motherhood for a while.

Now she was enjoying turning her hand to business again. In particular, working more closely with the foundation she and Mia had established. In conjunction with local businesses, they ran programmes to get vulnerable teens off the streets and into legitimate work or vocational training before they were lured into a life of crime they couldn't escape. Motivated by the tragic story of Luca's brother and also by the troubled teen who'd held Luca at gunpoint all those years ago, Annah and Mia had wanted to prevent other youths from stumbling down that same dark road.

Annah leaned in and pressed her mouth against Luca's, her chest swelling with the force of her emotions. Her feelings for her husband ran so deep they frightened her sometimes. But in those occasional moments when she felt overwhelmed by how much she adored and needed this man, she reminded herself she was stronger with Luca than without him.

And that wasn't weakness.

That was love.

* * * * *

If you enjoyed
The Sicilian's Secret Son
by Angela Bissell
you're sure to enjoy these other
Secret Heirs of Billionaires stories!

Married for His One-Night Heir
by Jennifer Hayward
The Secret Kept from the Italian
by Kate Hewitt
Demanding His Secret Son
by Louise Fuller
The Sheikh's Secret Baby
by Sharon Kendrick

Available now!

#3717 PENNILESS VIRGIN TO SICILIAN'S BRIDE
Conveniently Wed!
by Melanie Milburne
Gabriel offers a simple exchange—for her hand in marriage he'll save Francesca's ancestral home. And their attraction can only sweeten the deal. But her secret innocence is enough to make Gabriel crave his wife—forever!

#3718 WEDDING NIGHT REUNION IN GREECE
Passion in Paradise
by Annie West
When Emma overhears Christo admitting he married her for convenience, she flees, not expecting him to follow—with seduction in mind! Will a night in her husband's bed show Emma there's more than convenience to their marriage?

#3719 MARRIAGE BARGAIN WITH HIS INNOCENT
by Cathy Williams
Matias never does anything by halves. So when Georgie confesses his family believes they're engaged, he'll ensure everyone believes their charade. But discovering Georgie's true innocence suddenly makes their fake relationship feel unexpectedly—deliciously!—real...

#3720 BILLIONAIRE'S MEDITERRANEAN PROPOSAL
by Julia James
To convince everyone he's off-limits, Tara will pose as billionaire Marc's girlfriend. But when the world believes they're engaged, becoming his fiancée pushes their desire to new heights! Dare Tara believe their Mediterranean fantasy could be real?

HPCNM0419RB

To secure his heir, Alessio will use his incredible chemistry with his nephew's legal guardian, Beth, and command her to marry him! But will their intensely passionate marriage be enough for this innocent Cinderella?

Read on for a sneak preview of Michelle Smart's next story,
A Cinderella to Secure His Heir.

'Do not misunderstand me. Getting custody of Domenico is my primary motivation. He is a Palvetti and he deserves to take his place with us, his family. In my care he can have everything. But if custody were all I wanted, he would already be with me.'

She took another sip of her drink. Normally she hated whisky in any of its forms, but right then the burn it made in her throat was welcome. It was the fire she needed to cut through her despair. 'Then what do you want? I think of all the work we've done, all the hours spent, all the money spent—'

'I wanted to get to know you.'

She finally allowed herself to look at him. 'Why?'

The emerald eyes that had turned her veins to treacle lasered into hers. He leaned forward and spoke quietly. 'I wanted to learn about you through more than the reports and photographs my investigators provided me with.'

'You had me investigated?'

'I thought it prudent to look into the character of the person caring for my nephew.'

Her head spun so violently she felt dizzy with the motion.

He'd been spying on her.

She should have known Alessio's silence since she'd refused his offer of money in exchange for Dom had been ominous. She'd lulled herself into a false sense of security and underestimated him and underestimated the lengths he would be prepared to go to.

Everything Domenico had said about his brother was true, and more.

Through the ringing in her ears, he continued, 'Do not worry. Any childhood indiscretions are your own concern. I only wanted to know about the last five years of your life and what I learned about you intrigued me. It was clear to me from the investigators' reports and your refusal of my financial offer that you had an affection for my nephew…'

'Affection does not cover a fraction of the love I feel for him,' she told him fiercely.

'I am beginning to understand that for myself.'

'Good, because I will never let him go without a fight.'

'I understand that, too, but you must know that if it came to a fight, you would never win. I could have gone through the British courts and made my case for custody—I think we are both aware that my wealth and power would have outmatched your efforts—but Domenico is familiar with you and it is better for him if you remain in his life than be cut off.'

She held his gaze and lifted her chin. 'I'm all he knows.'

He raised a nonchalant shoulder. 'But he is very young. If it comes to it, he will adapt without you quickly. For the avoidance of doubt, I do not want that outcome.'

'What outcome do you want?'

'Marriage.'

Drumbeats joined the chorus of sound in her head. 'What on earth are you talking about?'

He rose from his seat and headed back to the bar. 'Once I have Domenico in Milan, it will be a simple matter for me to take legal guardianship of him.' He poured himself another large measure and swirled it in his glass. 'I recognise your genuine affection for each other and have no wish to separate you. In all our best interests, I am prepared to marry you.'

Dumbfounded, Beth shook her head, desperately trying to rid herself of all the noise in her ears so she could think properly. 'I wouldn't marry you if you paid me.'

Don't miss
A Cinderella to Secure His Heir.
Available May 2019 wherever
Harlequin® Presents books and ebooks are sold.

www.Harlequin.com